THE DEAD ARE DISCREET

THE JACOB ASCH MYSTERIES
BY ARTHUR LYONS

The Dead Are Discreet
All God's Children
The Killing Floor
Dead Ringer
Castles Burning
Hard Trade
At the Hands of Another

A JACOB ASCH MYSTERY

THE DEAD ARE DISCREET

ARTHUR LYONS

An Owl Book

HOLT RINEHART AND WINSTON
New York

Published by Holt, Rinehart and Winston,
383 Madison Avenue, New York, New York 10017.
Published simultaneously in Canada by Holt, Rinehart and
Winston of Canada, Limited.

Library of Congress Cataloging in Publication Data
Lyons, Arthur.
    The dead are discreet.
    (A Jacob Asch Mystery)
    "An Owl book."
    I. Title.   II. Series: Lyons, Arthur. Jacob Asch
mystery.
PS3562.Y446DA   1983   813'.54   83-103
ISBN 0-03-060393-5

First published in hardcover by Mason & Lipscomb
in 1974
First Owl Book Edition—1983

Printed in the United States of America
10 9 8 7 6 5 4 3 2 1

ISBN 0-03-060393-5

For Larry Larsen, private detective,
who showed me the ropes

And for Ray Bradbury, writer,
who was so free with his time and talent

Les morts
C'est discret,
Ça dort
Trop au frais.

Jules LaForgue
Complainte de l'oubli des moris

THE DEAD ARE DISCREET

CHAPTER 1

I didn't have much trouble finding Paul Ellman's new business address. It was one of those trim and sterile black glass monoliths that dwarf the colorful walks and shops of Century City. The last time I had worked a case for Paul, he had been located on the corner of Third and Broadway, just a hop, skip, and jump from the Hall of Justice, the New County Jail, and half a dozen all-night bail bondsmen. But about six months ago, Paul and his partner, Larry Steinberg, had decided to forsake convenience for appearance and had made the move. I couldn't blame them, really, not in this age of conspicuous consumption. It was just that it was a long haul from my own office.

I walked through the lobby, past an eight-foot-high metal sculpture that looked like a tornado in a junkyard, to the five pairs of stainless steel elevator doors that lined the marble wall opposite the entrance, and pressed the UP button. When I stepped out onto the fourth floor, my already-splitting head was ringing with the lilting, 46-violin version of "Shenandoah" I'd been treated to on the way up, and I groped my way down the hallway looking for Suite 409. I found it and went in.

The couch-lined waiting room was large and plushly decorated in soft browns and golds and the frosted hair of the receptionist blended right in. She looked up from her desk and smiled.

"May I help you?"

"I have an appointment with Mr. Ellman."

"Your name, please?"

"Jacob Asch."

"Just a minute, please." She picked up the phone and dialed two digits. "Mr. Asch is here to see you, Mr. Ellman. Yes. I'll tell him." She put the receiver back on its cradle. "Mr. Ellman will be with you in just a minute. If you'd like to sit down—"

"Thank you."

I sat down on one of the couches, feeling as if I could use an intravenous injection of aspirin, and tried to reconstruct the morning's telephone conversation with Paul. It seemed to me that the word "murder" had been mentioned once or twice, but I was still drawing a blank on the details. The entire conversation was wrapped in a dull fog, the kind of fog that rolls in after a quart of bourbon and three hours sleep. I hadn't told Paul that, of course. At least I hoped I hadn't. There was no sense for both of us to be edgy. Besides, I needed the work.

My efforts at recollection hadn't gotten very far when the door to my right opened and Paul Ellman walked out. He must have gained twenty pounds since the last time I had seen him. The new weight hung conspicuously on his jowls and that, combined with his bushy gray hair, gave him the appearance of an over-fed squirrel. The suit he was wearing was obviously expensive—blue silk, shiny and new—but had that slept-in look all of Paul's suits get after he has worn them once or twice. In contrast to his suit, his hands were clipped and slender and neat, the kind of hands that could deal perfect seconds and thirds and on more than one occasion, probably had.

He strode up to me smiling and clasped my hand firmly. Too firmly, in fact. When he let go, I uncurled my fingers slowly, feeling as if I wouldn't be able to dial a telephone for a week. But that was Paul; everything he did he overdid.

Paul and I had first met four years ago while I was still

working as a crime reporter for the *Chronicle*. I had been doing a series of articles on an armed robbery case in which he was an associate counsel, and during my research, I had dug up evidence that the prosecution's star eyewitness had been sixty miles away from the scene of the crime on the day in question. In the interest of justice, I passed on my information to Paul, and two hours after the "not guilty" verdict came in, he called me up and offered me a job as an investigator anytime I got tired of working for the paper.

He was stunned that day two years later when I sauntered into his office and told him I was ready to go to work. He had heard that I had been cited for contempt for refusing to reveal my news sources for the story I had done on the Lawson trial, but I guess he, like everybody else, had forgotten about me during the six months I had spent rotting in the New County Jail.

"Good to see you, Jake. You look like the wrath of God, as usual."

"Don't worry, it's not contagious."

"Pretty rough night?"

"The worst."

"Well, come into the office and sit down and you might feel better."

He led me into an olive-green and rosewood-panelled affair, the walls of which were filled by shelves of lawbooks and a few colorful, if not good, pieces of abstract art. I sat down in one of the leather easy chairs and he sat down at his desk.

"Looks like you've gained a little weight," he said. "Still doing the handball bit every morning?"

"I've been shirking the last couple of months. I've got to start again, though. I'm getting too far out of shape."

"It's easy to do," he said, slapping his stomach. "Last year, I used to jog a mile every morning before I came to work. Now I don't think I could jog around the block. I've

3

put on twenty pounds in four months. Do you believe that? Twenty pounds."

I said I didn't believe it, that it looked more like thirty and asked him why he wanted to see me.

His smile faded and he cleared his throat and began to swing methodically back and forth in his swivel chair, his fingertips lightly touching the edge of the desk. "You've heard about the Warren murders?"

Who hadn't? Sheila Toppinger Warren, socialite, daughter of steel magnate Henry L. Toppinger, found dead with her boyfriend, two-bit film producer Randy Folsom. Both had been shot through the head with a .38 and both had had their throats cut. The woman's arms were covered with cigarette burns. The police were saying it was a torture slaying. Her husband was picked up a few hours after the bodies were discovered and booked on suspicion of murder. "Only what I've read in the papers."

"I'm representing the husband, John Meyer Warren. I've handled a few minor criminal matters for him in the past —a couple of drunk-driving scrapes—and now he's hired me to handle the murder charge."

"You'd better dump him. If the D.A. doesn't convince the jury he's guilty, the newspapers probably will."

"I'm trying to get a gag ruling on it now. Judge Forrester, the son of a bitch, has refused so far, but I think he'll change his mind in a couple of weeks."

"By then it may be too late. Every venireman you'll get in that courtroom will have guilty in his mind."

"That's why I want you to start nosing around. This case is important to me, Jake. It could put me on top."

"Your ego is showing."

He smiled. "It always did, didn't it?"

"Yeah, it always did. But your chances might not be too good. From what I understand, the cops have got this one just about sewed up."

4

"That's just the trouble. The cops are so goddamn sure Warren did it simply because they've got themselves a nice, neat little package. Look, I don't have to tell you how they work. There are a lot of unsolved murders in this city and they don't particularly want two more. Murder is political business. There's been a lot of heat on the Chief and the D.A. and the Commissioner lately by local politicians about the inability of the police to handle the crime problem and they're not about to let go of their prime suspect in this one."

"How are things stacking up so far from your side?"

"Not too good. A lot of bad-looking circumstantial evidence. Warren and his wife were separated. They had been known to fight frequently—at times violently. He was known to have been terribly jealous and he knew about Folsom. He even once told Folsom in front of witnesses that if he ever caught him with his wife, he'd kill him. Warren's car was spotted by a neighbor driving up to the house around eleven and seen leaving quite hurriedly shortly thereafter. He had a gun registered to him—a .38 Smith & Wesson revolver—the same caliber as the murder weapon, and since there were no cartridge casings found at the scene, the police are assuming the weapon used on Sheila Warren and Folsom was a revolver."

"What about ballistics?"

"Warren claims he lost his gun a few months before the murders. There's no way to run a ballistics test on a missing gun."

I nodded. "How was entry gained into the house?"

"There were no signs of forcible entry, so whoever killed Mrs. Warren and Folsom either had a key or the doors were left open or they were let in by Mrs. Warren, which would indicate that either she or Folsom knew him. The cops are trying to say that Warren used his own house key to get into the house, but Warren claims that he didn't have a key, that

5

since a couple of months ago, his wife had changed the locks and refused to give him a key."

I shook my head. What Paul had said about the police was true enough. Like a meandering stream that finds the path of least resistance and takes it, cops often grabbed the most convenient visible suspect who happened to be around and built a case around him. But I had to admit that this time it looked like they had themselves a natural. "It doesn't sound like you're going to need me. Better spend Warren's money where it will do you some good—getting his appeal ready."

The soft brown eyes regarded me thoughtfully from beneath the heavy folds of skin that fell down from the brow to form the eyelids. "I don't think he did it, Jake. I want you to talk to him and tell me what you think, but I really don't think he did it."

"Why not?" I asked.

"For one thing, he says he didn't and I don't think he's that good a liar. I've explained to him that if he pled guilty, there would be a damn good chance we could get him off on two counts of Murder Two with a reduced sentence, but he says that he's innocent and that he won't plead guilty to something he didn't do."

"Two counts of Murder Two could get him twenty years or more. Maybe he figures that's too big a chunk of time to spend in the slammer and that he might as well shoot for the whole works."

"Could be, but I doubt it. I don't think he's got the guts for that kind of gamble. I think if he did it, he would take the safe way and go for Murder Two."

"You're fishing."

"Not really. I've defended lots of killers in my time. *And* prosecuted them. And I'm telling you that this murder and John Warren's personality don't fit together. They just don't mesh."

He paused and waited for me to say something and when I didn't, he went on. "Warren is from back East, the son of a wealthy glass manufacturer. He was sent out here several years ago by his father to handle a new plant they were opening on the West Coast. He's a typical high-society, spoiled-rotten, rich kid. He comes off brash and condescending, but that's a shallow act to cover up a deep-seated insecurity. He's never really handled anything on his own. He's always been afraid of responsibility and even in his father's business, he refused to wade in and soil his own hands by making decisions of any importance. He's always made sure that there was a buffer of managerial talent between him and the business to save himself from taking the blame for any wrong decisions. If anything went wrong, he'd merely put the blame on whoever made the decision, fire him, and hire somebody else to take his place. You should see him now. He's scared stiff. For the first time in his life, he's gotten himself into shit up to his eyebrows, and nobody—not even his father—can pull him out. He's pissing in his pants."

"Look, I'd be pissing in my pants, too. I don't see your point."

He leaned forward and pointed a finger at me. "You would if you *knew* him, that's my point. He's yellow. He wouldn't have been capable of murdering his wife and Folsom. Not in the way it was done. The killing was too close, too messy. On an outside chance—*way* outside—if he was mad enough—I mean totally enraged—he might have been able to pull the trigger of a gun, *if* he was far enough away, that is. But those two had their throats cut, and that takes more guts or a blood-lust that Warren doesn't have. Using a knife like that is a mark of responsibility. It would be way too personal for him to handle."

"So far your case stinks. What have you got that's tangible?"

7

"The keys. Warren gave me the names of several locksmiths he used to deal with and I checked them out. One of them, a Mr. Borak of Glenwood Lock and Key, told me that he'd changed the locks at the Warren house at Mrs. Warren's request about three months before the murder. It doesn't prove anything, of course. The doors could have been left open. Or Warren might have possibly gotten a duplicate made, though I don't see how. But it stands to reason that she wouldn't have given him a key when she'd changed the locks to keep him out. And the maid at the house told me that during the past few months, she had never seen John Warren use a key to get in, that he always rang the front doorbell."

"His wife could have let him in."

"Not likely. Not with Folsom there." He watched me for a few seconds, trying to read my face. "Look, Jake, I don't know all of the answers. But I do know that there were just too many weird things going on up at that house to jump to the conclusion that John Warren killed his wife."

"Weird how?"

"Sheila Warren was a member of the jet set. She had plenty of money and lots of time to do nothing but spend it, so she indulged in all sorts of odd little games. It hasn't hit the papers yet, and I don't know if it ever will—the big hush-hush is on—but the postmortems showed that both Sheila Warren and Randy Folsom were on DMT when they were murdered. The cops found a pipe on the living room coffee table in which was a burned-out residue of parsley they had soaked in the stuff and dried out and smoked. Not only that. They also found a nice supply of other assorted goodies in one of the bathroom medicine cabinets."

"What kind of goodies?"

"Some grass and hashish. Small quantities of heroin and cocaine. And a lot of belladonna."

"Belladonna. Their dope tastes were pretty exotic."

"Yeah. And it all fits in."

Another cue. Paul liked to give cues. It let him know that his audiences were still awake. I sighed and plunged ahead. "Fits in with what?"

"Belladonna is an hallucinogen traditionally used by witchcraft and black magic cults. According to John Warren, during the past year, his wife had started to take a rather unhealthy interest in the occult. That was apparently one reason for the breakup of their marriage—John insisted that she stop hanging around with the nuts she was keeping company with and she didn't like it. She was getting into the Southern California witchcraft scene pretty heavily from the picture he paints. He says he came home one afternoon about four months ago and found her burning incense and muttering some sort of litany in front of a piecemeal altar she had made in the living room. He kicked it over and a fight ensued. That was when she had the locks on the house changed."

"Interesting," I said, and meant it.

He took a sheet of paper from the folder that was lying on the desk and passed it over to me. "You want to see something really interesting, take a look at this."

The paper was a Xeroxed copy of some sort of diagram. The diagram consisted of two concentric circles and between the borders of the inner and outer circles were indecipherable scribblings and some hieroglyphic-like symbols. In the middle of the inner circle was a larger hieroglyph, dominating the rest. Outside the circles, on either side, were two Xs and the words "candlesticks," and across the bottom of the page was written: "outside diam. =9 ft., inside=7 ft."

"That was found drawn on the floor of the livingroom. Both bodies were found inside the circles. Where it says 'candlesticks' there, there were two brass, cobra-shaped candleholders complete with black candles."

9

"What in the hell is it?"

"Nobody seems to know. The symbols looked Egyptian to me, so I took the picture to a friend of mine who's an Egyptologist at UCLA and he said he'd never seen anything like it before, that it looked like a hodge-podge of Egyptian and western occult magic, but he confirmed that some of the symbols were from the Egyptian *Book of the Dead*. The one in the middle there is the symbol of Anubis, the jackal-headed lord of the cemetery, and the other four are the characters of his underlings, the genii of death."

"Charming. So what do your friends in the D.A.'s office think about this?"

"They think Sheila Warren and Folsom were holding some sort of far-out ritual when they were interrupted by the killer—namely, John Warren."

"But you think they're all wet."

"I've already told you I don't think he did it."

"What about the neighbor who saw Warren's car coming and going on the night of the murder?"

"Warren admits he went up there that night, but he says he got there after the murders had happened. He says he found the front door open, walked in, found the lights off, and tripped over the body of his wife. Then he got scared and left. That's his version, and that's the version I'm going to believe until somebody convinces me otherwise."

I shrugged. "You're paid to believe him."

"Look, Jake, there's more to this case that smells besides Mrs. Warren's preoccupation with the occult. I've been checking around, and Randy Folsom had a reputation as being quite a sexual deviant. He went any way that was available, and from the stories I've heard, the kinkier the better. He was producing underground films—artsy-craftsy stuff—up to about six or seven years ago, but flopped and started cranking out porno."

"Think there might be some connection there?"

"I don't know. All I know is that there are too many loose ends the cops aren't bothering to tie up. They've got their sacrificial lamb to placate the public with, so they aren't looking any farther." He put both hands flat on the desk and leaned forward, as if he were going to say something very, very important. "You know why I want you on this thing with me, Jake?"

Here it came. "No, why?"

"Because you've got balls. And I'm going to need somebody with balls on this case. Somebody who isn't afraid."

I held up a hand. "Save the pitch for the jury, Paul. You want me on this case because you want somebody who can wade through it up to his eyeballs and not puke from the smell."

"Jesus Christ, there's no need to get touchy. I was only paying you a compliment."

"Spare me the compliments. I've heard them all before. I'll take your money, Paul. Just don't try to tie any colored ribbons to it."

"What's eating you this morning?"

What could I tell him? That the day the whole Lawson mess broke open old man Simon had pulled me into his office and paid me that same "compliment" and that I had had to learn through a messenger boy two weeks later that I had been canned and that the *Chronicle* was refusing to back me up on the contempt of court charge and that what was eating me this morning was the same thing that had been eating me for the last two years and that he had innocently but clumsily triggered it off once again? It was beginning to sound a bit stale, even to me.

"Nothing. Forget it. I'm just kind of edgy. This headache is really something."

"Sure."

"Look, I could use a retainer. I'm tap city right now."

"Five hundred do it?"

I nodded.

He pulled a checkbook out of his desk drawer, scribbled in it, ripped out a check and handed it to me.

"Now when can I see John Warren?"

CHAPTER 2

I drove downtown and met Ellman in the parking lot across from the County Jail. Walking up the steps to the big, blocky, gray concrete abortion made me slightly uneasy. It always did. There was always the vague, nagging feeling in the back of my mind that once inside, they would slam the doors shut behind me, and this time never let me out.

Inside the big glass doors, visitors milled around, waiting their turn to see friends or relatives. Old faces, young faces, long-hairs, short-hairs, whites, blacks, browns, women with armloads of kicking, struggling children and women with no children at all, sat waiting on hard wooden benches for a chance to pick up the telephone receiver on the wall that separated the Inside from the Outside and talk to a face that stared back through four-inch-thick glass plate.

A line of people had formed at the information desk where a uniformed black policewoman was taking names and stabbing buttons on a computer remote. "Before seeing a prisoner," she shouted to the crowd, "you *must* have a booking number. You must supply the prisoner's *complete* name in order to get the proper booking number—"

Nobody paid much attention to her and people continued to shout names and she continued to stab buttons. We walked past a couple of uniformed sheriffs and plain-clothesmen who were standing by the desk giving the crowd the Evil Eye, and into a small foyer. A wooden bench lined one wall of the foyer and on it, a man was sitting by himself. I didn't know what he was waiting for, but it looked like the end of the world.

Ellman walked over to the ledge that was on the opposite wall, filled out a small white visitor's form and handed me one to fill out. After supplying the answers on the card, I handed it back to him and he went over and tapped on the glass cage in which a young sheriff was sitting with his nose in a copy of *True Life Detective*. He looked up as if the knock had startled him and reached over to slide open the window.

"Paul Ellman to see John Warren. This is my investigator, Jacob Asch."

We both showed him our I.D.'s and he took our forms. The thick steel door swung open and the cop behind it pushed it closed and locked it after us. After a cursory search, we were admitted into the Attorney Room.

The room was large and painted an ugly, high-gloss, blue-gray color. Rows of long tables ran its length and seated at them between numbered glass partitions, lawyers and their prisoner-clients discussed the progress of their various cases.

"I've requested a private conference room," Paul said to the cop who'd searched us.

"Take number four. I'll call upstairs and have them bring him down."

Paul nodded and walked toward one of the sound-proofed glass booths that lined the far wall. We went in and sat down to wait.

John Meyer Warren, escorted by a guard, made his appearance shortly. He was dressed in jailhouse denims. He was tall and everything about him seemed thin. Thin long legs, thin sandy hair, thin pointed nose, thin hard lips. Even the veneer of age that covered his face was thin. Behind it there was something that had failed to mature with the march of time.

14

The guard left the booth and shut the door and Warren and I shook hands after a brief introduction by Paul. He pulled up a chair and watched me circumspectly as I whipped out a notepad and a pen.

"Before we start," Paul said to him, "I must warn you again to be careful of what you say. These rooms are supposed to be clean, but I wouldn't want to take any chances. You never know who might be listening."

"It's all right," Warren answered sullenly. "I told you I've got nothing to hide."

I looked into the eyes that were heavy and pink-rimmed from lack of sleep. They were an insipid brown, the pale amber of a glass of scotch. Through their translucence, I thought I saw something helpless and trapped that urgently demanded pity, and I felt myself reacting against the demand. I looked away toward Paul, who was quietly going through some of his notes, and when I looked back, the eyes were blank.

"Before we get into anything, Mr. Warren, let me explain one thing. Any criminal investigation has to be aimed in a certain direction; otherwise a lot of time and effort is inevitably wasted. I know you've already gone over this with Paul, but if I dig up facts for one defense tactic and if that tactic turns out to be the wrong one, most likely it will be completely obliterated in court by a good prosecutor. A lot of cases that might have been salvaged have been lost that way."

"What are you trying to say?"

"Simply this. Paul tells me that you've told him that you're innocent. There is a lot of bad—and I mean *bad*—circumstantial evidence pointing to your guilt. Now if I start digging up facts, for your sake they'd better be the right facts. Finding material to prove your innocence is going to be one thing and digging up material to bolster a plea of Murder Two would be quite another."

15

"You're asking me if I murdered my wife."

"That's what I'm asking you."

He looked down at the tips of his fingers which rested limply on his knees. The nails were down to the quick and the skin around them was pretty well chewed. He slapped his knees hard, then looked up at me. "No, I didn't kill my wife, okay? We had our troubles, sure. But I loved Sheila and I know she loved me. I went up there that night to see if I could patch things up. I got there after it happened. They were both dead when I got there. That's the truth."

"Tell me exactly what happened that night."

He took a deep breath, felt the palms of his hands, then rubbed them on his pants. "I left the plant about six and went over to get some dinner at Stu's on La Cienega. I was in a foul mood, and I sat around there drinking until about ten. Then I got in my car and drove around for a while, not knowing really where I was going. At least that's what I thought. I guess I really did, though, because I wound up at the house."

"What time was that?"

"It must have been around eleven or so."

"You said earlier that you went over to try to patch things up."

"That's right."

"How could that be if you didn't know where you were going?"

He jumped up and pushed back his chair. He looked hurt. "What the hell is this? I thought you were here to help me, not give me the goddamn third degree."

"I am getting information, Mr. Warren, in the best way I know how. If there are inconsistencies in your story, I've got to iron them out."

He sat back down, but the resentment was still in his face. "Okay, okay. I realized that that was what I was doing *after* I got there. You know how it is, you try to fool yourself, you

16

keep telling yourself that you're just taking a drive to take a drive when you know deep down that's a lie. I was going over to beg her to come back to me. I thought—I don't know if it was the drinks or what, that if I could just reason with her and show her how foolish she was being, that she was being victimized by that son of a bitch, that she'd come back to me."

"You knew Folsom was there when you went over?"

"Yes. Sheila changed the locks on the house because I knew. I told her I'd kill him if I caught them together."

"What happened when you got to the house?"

"I went to the front door and found it partially open. I thought that was strange because Sheila was always meticulous about locking the doors. It was one thing she was almost fanatical about. Anyway, the house was dark when I came in—but I could see a faint glow coming from the living room. I called, but nobody answered, so I went on in. There were candles burning on the floor and the room was filled with the heavy smell of burning incense. I immediately thought Sheila was playing one of her silly occult games again, and started for the light switch. That was when I tripped over something big and fell.

"I was lucky the furniture had been cleared away from the center of the room; otherwise I probably would have hit my head on something. Anyway, I got up and turned on the lights and saw that I'd tripped over a body. Then I saw the other one. They were lying close to each other, their hands were tied behind their backs, and they had black hoods over their heads. There was blood everywhere. It was horrible. I stumbled outside and threw up and then I got out of there as fast as I could."

He stuck one of the ragged fingers in his mouth and began to gnaw on it.

"Why didn't you call the police?"

"I was scared. The blood, everything scared me. Then I

17

knew they would think I did it. So I took off."

"Did you take off the hoods from the bodies to take a look at the faces?"

"No. I knew who it was."

"You reportedly had a .38 caliber Smith & Wesson revolver registered to you, Mr. Warren. Where is it now?"

"I don't know. I haven't seen it in months. I might have left it in the house before I moved out."

"The police didn't find it there."

"Look, Asch, I told you I don't know where it is."

I nodded. "How long had you been married?"

"Seven years. Sheila and I had known each other in Boston in college. We got married after we both graduated."

"When did you first start having marital difficulties?"

"About two years ago. Her little brother was killed in Vietnam and Sheila was quite upset about it. She started consulting some charlatan medium that some of her friends used to get psychic readings from, to try to contact Jimmy. That was her dead brother—Jimmy. She started going to seances. She claimed to me that it was just entertainment, but I knew she was really starting to believe in all that crap. That was when I put my foot down and told her that she would have to get a grip on herself. I suggested that she start visiting a psychiatrist."

"What did she say to that?"

"She hit the ceiling. Told me that if anybody was nuts, it was me and that I could go to hell with my psychiatrists. I never mentioned it again, but from that time on there was a strain in our relationship that got steadily worse. Then she came to me one day and said she intended to sue me for a divorce. I told her that she should cool off and think about it. I promised to give her the house if she didn't initiate any hasty action. She agreed to a trial separation, and I let her live in the house. But she took up with that scum Folsom—God knows what she saw in him—and decided to go ahead with the divorce. He moved into the house with her."

"Do you happen to remember the name of the medium your wife visited?"

"No. I know she used to go to séances out in Altadena somewhere. But that was over a year ago."

"Mmmmmm. Paul tells me that your wife was also dabbling in witchcraft."

He threw a glance at Paul that looked as if it were supposed to mean something, but Ellman didn't catch it. "Yeah. That was more recently. She was hanging around with one girl who claimed to be a witch. I met her once at the house a few months ago when I came up to see Sheila. Her name was Sascha. She sold herbs or something like that at some psychedelic shop off Hollywood Boulevard. Isis was the name of the place."

"What about the incident with the altar?"

"I came in one afternoon and found Sheila kneeling in front of the living room coffee table holding some sort of ceremonial dagger. I kicked over the table and took the dagger out of her hand and threw it in the corner. She went crazy. Tried to claw my face and I hit her. I went down to Isis that afternoon and told Sascha that if she didn't stay away from my wife, I was going to have her prosecuted for fraud."

"So what did this Sascha say?"

"Nothing. She just sat there smiling."

I flipped over another page of my notebook and set the pen down on it. "Any other strange people you know about that your wife was hanging around with?"

"There were others, but I never met them. Sheila always made sure of that. She knew how hostile I was to her associating with such people."

"Did your wife have any relatives or close friends out here on the Coast?"

19

"She had friends. As far as relatives, she has a sister who lives in Bel Air. Her name is Gloria Pilsen. Lives at 904 Lambretta Drive. But you'd just be wasting your time talking to her. She'd just tell you that I killed Sheila."

"You two don't get along?"

"That bitch doesn't get along with anybody."

He looked down at the floor and when he looked back up, his eyes were moist. The demand was there again. The kid had run the gamut of emotions, as any kid will under strain, from self-pity to despair to frustration to anger to hostility and back again to self-pity. We had come full circle and neither of us wanted to start the circle again, so I stood up.

"Well, Mr. Warren, this should give me a start anyway. I'd like you to make out a list of all the people you can remember that were friends of your wife—close friends, acquaintances, anybody you can think of. Give it to Paul and he'll get it to me. If I need any more information, I'll come back."

Ellman signalled through the glass to the guard, who came in and stood silently as Paul gave his assurances to Warren that the case was building up nicely and that with old Asch on the job, something was bound to break soon because I was the best investigator in the whole wide world. The praise was still ringing in my ears when the steel door closed behind us, choking off the muted conversations that filled the blue-gray room.

"Well?" Paul asked as we walked out to the cars.

"Well what?"

"What do you think?"

"It doesn't matter what I think. You didn't hire me to give you an instant character analysis, just information."

"Try giving me an instant character analysis."

"I don't like him, if you must know, but that doesn't mean anything. If you want to know if I think that Warren is the murderer type, I'd have to say that when it comes to your wife shacking up with another man, there is no murderer type."

"You think he's guilty."

"I didn't say that. I'm just saying that I didn't see him the night of the murder when he went into that house. I see him now. What I see is a kid who never really grew up because he was spoiled and overprotected and who's scared of being put into prison for the rest of his life, over which I really can't blame him. I would agree with you on one point, though. I don't think a knife would be his weapon. If he was going to kill anybody I think he would have used a gun."

A small, crooked smile of triumph passed across his lips. "Going to your office?"

"No. I've got some things that I can take care of while I'm over here. I've got to have more to go on than witches and ghosts. Oh, by the way, if you want to save me some time and yourself some money, tell your secretary to write to the Department of Motor Vehicles in Sacramento and ask for a complete driving history for both Sheila Warren and Folsom. If I have to do it, I'll charge you for stationery, wear on my typewriter ribbon, a new manicure for the fingernails I chip typing it and gas to get over to the office."

He shook his head and grinned. "For an honest man you certainly are outrageous."

"Yep. And for an affluent man you certainly are cheap."

We split up in the parking lot, the honest man heading for his dusty, four-year-old 90,000-mile Plymouth and the cheap man for his brand-new gold Cadillac Eldorado.

21

CHAPTER 3

I hadn't had a thing to eat since yesterday, so I grabbed a fast hamburger at a street stand before going over to the public library to look through the newspaper accounts of the murders. There was nothing in the papers I didn't already have. I combed later articles that covered the funerals of both Mrs. Warren and Randy Folsom and made a list of names of those in attendance.

After leaving the library, I skipped over to the County Clerk's office and ran through their Superior and Municipal court files to determine whether either of the victims had had any criminal or civil suits brought against him while he was alive.

Mrs. Warren was clean, but there were several interesting entries under Folsom's name. One, dated February 6, 1965, showed Folsom's name and a bail number, B-123096. Nothing after that, which probably meant that he had been picked up on a felony, not charged within the legal seventy-two hours, then released. There were also two other case numbers under his name, one a criminal action in 1970 and another a civil action in 1969.

The 1970 case turned out to be statutory rape and contributing to the delinquency of a minor charges filed against Folsom and a man named William K. Jeffries. It seemed that a Mr. and Mrs. Frank W. Essen had claimed that Folsom and Jeffries had seduced their sixteen-year-old daughter and had recorded the seduction on film. Folsom and Jeffries had been arraigned on the charges and had

22

undergone a preliminary hearing, but at the trial the D.A. had asked for the charges to be dropped due to "insufficient evidence" and in the "interest of justice." The file had no address for Jeffries, but gave his date of birth, 8-2-38. I was luckier with the Essens—they had given their address as 1641 Claymoor Street, Santa Monica.

The other case that intrigued me was a civil suit brought against Folsom by the Filmways Equipment Rental Company for rental fees amounting to $2,500. This case had also been dropped, the parties having evidently settled out of court. It seemed that Folsom had had a talent for getting himself out of scrapes. I jotted down all the information I needed and left, deciding that I still had time to make it over to Bel Air to pay a visit to Mrs. Warren's sister.

Lambretta Drive snaked through the green hills of Bel Air with tall stone walls and lush, sloping lawns lining both its sides. Well shaded by tall trees, the air on the street was cool and moist and smelled of freshly mowed grass. The Pilsen house was not visible from the road, but I got the 904 from the post by the open gates and headed up the driveway.

After a couple of miles the dense green foliage that formed a canopy over the driveway cleared and I found myself pulling up to the front door of the house. It was a very old and very elegant two-story colonial-style mansion that looked like it had just been flown in from a Louisiana bayou. It had expansive white walls and great white pillars rising out of the brick porch by the front door. A silver Rolls sat majestically in front of the door. I pulled my Plymouth up behind it and killed the engine.

As I walked up the brick walkway, a Japanese gardener who was giving a manicure to the hedges with a large pair of clippers, yanked off his sweat-stained canvas hat and wiped his brow with a forearm. He said good afternoon and when he smiled, his eyes turned into two slits. I couldn't separate the eye-slits from the wrinkles in his face, but I said good afternoon back anyway. I looked around, wondering where the man's truck was and then remembered that this was the type of house where such unsightly vehicles as gardener's trucks were stowed far out of sight. I got a sudden twinge of self-consciousness about my Plymouth, but I didn't go back to move it.

After the second ring, the door opened and a small brown face appeared.

"I'd like to see Mrs. Pilsen, please," I said, handing her my card.

"Un momentito, por favor," she said and closed the door again. She was back within half a minute, waving me inside.

The entrance hall was immense, the ceiling being at least twenty feet above us. The heels of my shoes made lonely sounds against the black-and-white checkered tile floor. I was led through an archway that ran underneath the staircase and into a large living room. Gloria Pilsen was there, bending over a glass serving tray and pouring from a pitcher what looked like a martini.

She was tall and slender and her white slacks and blue turtleneck sweater fit her as they would a high-fashion model—attractively, but not seductively. Her dark brown hair hung unbound and long around her shoulders. Her eyes and mouth were large and well-set and sensual, unlike the rest of her body, which was too thin to be voluptuous. When she turned and smiled, her eyes said things. One of the things they said was that the martini in her hand was not the first one she had had today.

"My, my, you are a handsome one, aren't you? Actually, when I saw the name on the card, I expected somebody who looked more Jewish."

"Really? What does a Jew look like, Mrs. Pilsen?"

"Don't take offense. The remark wasn't meant to be a racial slur. I have nothing against the Jews. As a matter of

24

fact, my second husband, Arnold, was a Jew."

I felt like I should whip out the pennants and break into a cheer.

"It's the eyes that do it, you know. They're so blue."

"I've got a pair of dark glasses out in the car, if they disturb you."

"No, no. I love them, really. It's just that they're so coldly Aryan. Martini?"

"No thanks."

"Something else, perhaps?"

"No thanks."

"Well, won't you sit down and tell me what I can do for you?"

She sat down on the edge of a beige settee and I sat down on a chair facing her.

"I'm here about your sister, Mrs. Pilsen."

"Yes, of course. I took that for granted. What is it you'd like to know."

"I'm working for Paul Ellman."

She ran a long tapered finger slowly around the rim of her glass. "Yes, I heard John had hired Paul Ellman. You can tell Mr. Ellman that he's wasting his time. John's guilty as hell."

"Mr. Warren said that you'd probably say that. He said you didn't like him much."

She smiled a faint wisp of a smile. "He said that, really? Well, that's true, in a way, I suppose. I don't like him much. But I don't dislike him much, either. I don't feel anything about John one way or another. Emotionally, he draws a big fat zero with me. But that isn't why I say he did it."

"No? Why then?"

"Because he's weak. I told Sheila before she married him that it wouldn't work out. I knew John wouldn't be resilient enough to handle it. I knew he'd crack under the strain and something terrible would happen. To go through an emo-

25

tional storm as severe as a bad marriage, you've got to have a great deal of strength and a great deal of flexibility, don't you see. John had neither. My first husband was like John, to a T. Immature and much too emotional. Sheila needed somebody much stronger."

"What happened to your first husband?"

"He broke under the strain. Got despondent one night and drove his car off the end of a pier. I knew Sheila's marriage would wind up the same way—with one of them going off a pier. You see, Mr. Asch, although I wasn't very close to my sister, I knew her very well. I knew her because she was very much like me. That, in fact, is probably why I disliked her."

I wondered if she were pulling this last bit of psychology from sessions with her analyst or from the decanter of martinis on the tray in front of her.

"My bluntness doesn't shock you, does it?"

"Should it?"

"I don't know. A good many people would be shocked, I suppose."

"Very little shocks me any more."

"Good."

"How many times have you been married, Mrs. Pilsen?"

She took another sip from her drink and smiled. "Four. Married and divorced four times and I'm thirty-seven years old. But I'm resilient enough to handle it, you see. That's the secret."

I could see why John Warren wasn't crazy about his sister-in-law. If you took her seriously, it could rub you raw in a matter of minutes. Myself, I had seen it too many times in too many places to be moved to that strong a reaction. People are like inner tubes—inflate their egos with a little air and you really get to see where all the leaks are. Gloria Pilsen had been pumped up and was losing air fast. With people like her, living was a constant race to see if they could find another source of air before they went completely flat. Very few made it to the finish line.

"Are you married, Mr. Asch?"

"No."

"Ever been?"

"Once."

"And what happened, if I'm not prying."

I knew she didn't care if she was prying or not. "She didn't like being a reporter's wife. The hours finally got to her. She couldn't stand being left alone late at night. So, she found somebody with more regular hours. A doctor. They never make house calls anymore."

"You used to be a reporter?"

"Yes."

"What made you give up being a reporter and become a private detective?"

"I don't mean to be rude, Mrs. Pilsen, but I didn't come here to discuss me. I came to find out about your sister."

"I was just trying to find out more about Jacob Asch, that's all. After all, you wouldn't want me to divulge all of my well-kept family secrets to a total stranger now, would you?"

I didn't answer, but watched her poke at an ice cube that was floating in her glass with a highly polished fingernail. The cube bobbed and weaved, trying to escape her touch, but she relentlessly pursued it around the edge of the glass. I was beginning to know how that ice cube felt. She looked up.

"Not very communicative, are you?"

"I don't learn things by talking, just listening. I'm a trained listener. Now, Mrs. Pilsen, can you think of anybody besides John Warren who would have wanted to kill your sister?"

"Not really. In order to want to kill someone you would have to hate him and in order to hate him, you'd have to

27

get close to him. My sister never let anyone get that close to her. She was what you would call—uh—distant, keeping everybody at arm's length, even those who tried to love her. That was the one tragic character flaw that marked my sister's life. Except Jimmy, maybe. In a way, I suppose that distance was kind of a blessing—Sheila's death didn't leave too much grief behind. Nobody was close enough to her to really miss her. The only one I can think of who's truly sad about her death is my father, and he's more upset about the possibility of scandal than anything else."

"You mentioned Jimmy. I presume you meant your brother."

"Yes."

"What was the relationship between your brother and sister?"

She got up and went to the decanter to fill her empty glass. When she sat back down, she stared past me into the room beyond, as if she were trying to focus her vision on something far away. "They were very close. When my father and mother got divorced, we kids were split up and I went with mother while Jimmy and Sheila went with my father. Of course, since his primary interest was his businesses, Daddy never had much time for them and left the upbringing primarily to nurses and nannies. As a result, they were thrown that much closer together. Jimmy became a first lieutenant in the Army and happened to step on a landmine over in Vietnam. Daddy, being a true-blooded Christian American, wouldn't stand for any son of his to be buried on heathen soil, so he had the pieces gathered up and shipped back for burial.

"He should have let them bury him over there. The whole thing shook Sheila up pretty badly. She couldn't believe that Jimmy was really gone and the funeral sort of crystallized things for her. She had a nervous breakdown shortly afterward and wound up spending a year in a sanitarium. When she got out, she started getting interested in the supernatural—spiritualism—in an attempt to contact Jimmy. She was convinced that he was floating around up there somewhere in the ether. One day she called me on the phone, almost frantic, at about two in the morning, and told me she had made contact with Jimmy and that he was all right and happy. She said she knew it was he because he'd told her things—about a secret hideout they'd had when they were kids, down by the lake at the country house—that the medium couldn't possibly have known about."

"When was this?"

"Over a year ago."

"Do you remember the name of the medium?"

She waved a hand in the air. "What in the hell was it? Haskell? No. Harnell—that's it. Had some spiritualist church over in Altadena called the Church of Universal Wisdom. At least I think that was the name of it."

"Did you ever go to one of the seances with her?"

"No. I don't happen to believe in goblins and ghosts and things that go bump in the night—at least *those* things that go bump in the night." Her lips parted slightly, in what I assumed she thought was a seductive smile. It might have worked, but I wasn't in the mood.

"Did you ever have this Harnell checked out?"

"What for? What my sister wanted to do with her time and money was her own business."

"Did you ever meet Randy Folsom?"

"Only once. As I said, Sheila and I didn't communicate very much. But one night she came up here with Folsom and asked me to come with them. She said that she'd met this girl who was a witch who did fabulous tarot card readings. She said she'd been invited to a meeting of this witch's coven or whatever they call it and asked me if I wanted to go along."

"Did you go?"

"Of course not. I told her it was childish and I had better things to do."

"When was this?"

"Maybe seven, eight months ago. After she started to get hooked on the supernatural thing."

"One more question, Mrs. Pilsen. Who stands to inherit your sister's part of your father's will now that she's dead?"

"Why, Mr. Asch, you're a horrible man," she said, grinning. "I suppose I do, if you really want to know. But Daddy's as healthy as a mule. Pity. He's not likely to go for another ten or fifteen years, and by that time I'll be too old to enjoy it. Besides, if you're looking for a motive there, forget it. I'm still trying to figure out ways to spend my last husband's money. As a matter of fact, maybe you can help me. Are you a good thinker?"

"Fantastic. Call me after I finish this case."

"I don't know if I can wait that long. You're not going so soon?" she asked, seeing that I had stood up.

"Not if you can think of anything that might be important."

"Well, for starters, you could stop wasting your time and spend it more profitably."

"How?" I knew what was coming, but I thought I might as well ask the question anyway.

There was a coquettish glint in her eye, subtle, like a hungry wolf moving in for the kill. "You could have a martini with me."

"I'm afraid you'd be too much for a simple man like me to handle, Mrs. Pilsen."

"Gloria. I can't stand to be called Mrs. Pilsen. It reminds me of Roger. And if there's one thing I can't stand being reminded of, it's Roger."

"Okay, Gloria."

"That's better. And you don't seem to me to be all that simple, Mr. Asch."

"Jake. But I am. And you're a very scary woman, Gloria. Any woman who's had four husbands has got to be a little frightening."

She threw back her head and laughed, then made a sweeping gesture toward the room with her hand. "Surely all this could overcome some of your cowardice. Look at what you might get as a door prize. You never know, you could turn out to be Number Five."

"It's not against my principles to marry for money," I said, "but somehow I don't think I'd be resilient enough to handle you. I'll probably be talking to you, Gloria. Don't get up, I'll find my way out."

I left her there in the living room with her thoughts and her martini and the dying light of afternoon.

CHAPTER 4

The next morning, I looked up the Church of Universal Wisdom in the Altadena telephone book. Gloria Pilsen had remembered the name right. I called and made an appointment to see the pastor of the church, the Reverend James Harnell.

The church was located on a small side street, the only other building on the block being a large, drab-gray low-rent apartment building. The rest of the street was vacant dirt lots resplendent with weeds. The church was a converted one-story house surrounded by banana plants.

A sign by the door read: SUNDAY SERVICES 10:00 A.M. SEANCES TUES. THURS. 9:00 P.M.

A chunky, heavy-faced woman answered the door. A wilted corsage of red flowers decorated her pink dress. She didn't seem particularly disturbed by the fact that the flowers were dying; she was probably comforted by her certain knowledge that they would soon be happy in Flower Heaven.

"You must be Mr. Asch," she said, smiling abundantly.

I smiled back, but I'm sure my Abundance Rating would have been only a C-.

"I'm Mrs. Nielsen, Reverend Harnell's secretary. I talked with you on the phone earlier this morning. You're a little early."

"A few minutes. I wanted to give myself a little leeway to find the place."

"Well, the Reverend is in consultation right now, but should be finished shortly. Won't you sit down?"

I thanked her and stepped inside. The room had obviously once been the living room of the house. Metal folding chairs were set up in neat rows facing a small elevated stage up front which was surrounded by pink and white wreaths of plastic flowers. In back of the stage was a large cross painted on the wall into which the words PEACE and HARMONY were written horizontally and vertically, the A of PEACE being the A of HARMONY. Mrs. Nielsen, still smiling, showed me to one of the folding chairs and beckoned me to sit down. She offered me a glass of lemonade which I politely declined, and after buzzing around me for a few minutes, excused herself apologetically. She said that there was work she must get done and that the Reverend would be in momentarily. She would tell him I was here. She thanked me again for being so patient and left. A nice woman, Mrs. Nielsen.

It wasn't too long after she left the room that I heard footsteps and muffled voices, and from the hallway to my left, a tall man appeared with his arm gently wrapped like a shawl around the shoulders of an elderly, white-haired lady. The man had a gaunt landscape of a face, the cheeks looking as if they had been scooped out for economy. His hair was jet black except where it was turning white around the temples, and it looked even blacker in contrast to the extremely pale, almost blue-white color of his skin. His forehead was high and prominent, sloping down to form a ledge above the eyes and a single, unbroken black line of eyebrow ran along the ledge, delineating where the eyes began and the forehead ended.

"Don't you worry, Mrs. Galworthy," he was saying soothingly into the ear of the woman as he led her toward the front door. "We will make contact with your husband at the

33

seance on Thursday. Conditions look very favorable. And from the signs you tell me about, it appears certain that he's trying very hard to reach you. I don't anticipate any problems at all."

She gave him a few worried thank-yous and assured him that she would be there on Thursday. Once she was out the door, he turned and strode over to me. I stood up and we shook hands.

"Sorry to hold you up, Mr. Asch. Let's go back to my office."

He led me back through the doorway and down a narrow hallway, into a small room. He sat behind the desk and I took one of the chairs.

"Now what exactly did you want to see me about?"

I pulled out my wallet and showed him my private investigator's license. "I'm working on the Warren murders, Reverend."

Something stirred in his eyes, a sign that flashed DAN-GER for a split second, almost undetectable before it faded. "And?"

"I thought you might be able to answer a few questions."

He shifted in his chair. "Why would you come to me?"

"Because Mrs. Warren used to attend seances at this church. Quite often, from what I understand."

He cleared his throat and folded his hands on the desk top, staring pensively at the pink fingernails that adorned the ends of the long, blue-white fingers. "I won't deny that Mrs. Warren was a frequent visitor to the church. She came for consultations quite often. But that was quite a while ago, and she stopped coming at least a year ago. I don't know how anything I could tell you would be any help to your investigation." He stared at me thoughtfully, then sucked on the insides of his cheeks, making the sunken hollows turn an odd gray color. "Frankly, Mr. Asch, I'm reluctant to answer your questions simply because I have an entire congregation to protect. I knew someone would eventually come to me about Mrs. Warren, of course. It was inevitable. But I have been dreading the day. You see, spiritualism gets enough adverse publicity as it is without being tied up with notorious murder cases. Because of the nature of our beliefs, we are constantly being subjected to the petty harrassment of police and journalists who see good copy in exposing a fraudulent medium or depicting us as kooks simply because we are outside the mainstream of religious thought."

"I'm not here to expose anybody as a fraud or ridicule anybody's religious beliefs, Reverend Harnell. I'm here to get information on Mrs. Warren. There is a man with his life at stake here. I'm sure you can realize the gravity of the situation."

He sat quietly for a minute. "Yes, of course. I'm sorry. What do you wish to know?"

"Why she was coming here."

"She wanted to contact her dead brother who was killed in Vietnam. She was curious about the Other Side, as are all people who come here."

"Who acted as the medium for Mrs. Warren?"

"I did."

"And you reached her brother?"

"Yes."

"How do you know it was her brother you reached?"

"I don't have to. Mrs. Warren knew. There were certain incidents the spirit related—childhood experiences that nobody else could have known about, certainly not I. I've never had any contact with the family at all, aside from Mrs. Warren, and she never related anything about her childhood to me."

"Did you notice anything peculiar about Mrs. Warren?"

His gaze darkened. "Peculiar? How do you mean?"

Then I realized the nature of the communications break-down. It was the word "peculiar." An ordinary word with a simple meaning. Peculiar—strange, out of the ordinary. But to him the word was a nasty insinuation.

"I mean anything about her behavior that struck you as being abnormal? Was she the same as all your other members? Did she have any odd quirks that might have stood out in your mind?"

Recollections moved across his face swiftly, like steel balls in a pinball machine trying to hit the 500-point pocket. "Well, she was a very nervous and high-strung woman, for one thing. The people we get approaching us are under-standably nervous about death, but her nervousness was of a different nature. Most of our members are over forty. We do have some younger members, but they usually come more out of curiosity than anything else, and they aren't what you'd call steadies. It's strange for someone as young as Mrs. Warren to have been so preoccupied with death. With her, death seemed to be an obsession. She took it very seriously. Too seriously, maybe."

"Why?"

"Thoughts of death are too distant for a young person to be bothered with, and that's the way it should be. It's only after a certain age that mundane affairs begin to seem less important and the eternal questions of the meaning of life and death assume more and more importance. Do you follow me?"

"I think so."

"Talk to any of our members and you'll see that they all carry around with them an inner peace. You met Mrs. Nielsen? Two years ago, after her husband died, she came to us in a state of almost total nervous collapse. She had been married thirty years and in one night it had all been

36

torn from her. She was beside herself. She didn't know where to turn. Look at her now. Since our members are certain about what will come in the future life, they aren't bothered by fears of death. But Mrs. Warren never reached that point of inner peace. She longed to know, she was driven by the inner compulsion to know more about death, but she never really accepted the answers, even after she made contact with her brother. I suppose that's why she left us."

"How much did it cost her to contact her brother?"

He smiled at me benevolently. "Don't worry, your question doesn't offend me. Your skepticism is quite understandable. As I said before, since the bereaved are in a suggestible state after the death of a loved one, they are often easy prey for unscrupulous mediums. But those mediums are usually independents. The Church of Universal Harmony is a member of the National Amalgamation of Spiritualist Churches, a national organization which acts as a sort of supervisory board for all its member churches. I am a licensed medium with the N.A.S.C. There are very strict prerequisites for mediumship in the Amalgamation, and fraudulent activity is not tolerated. Taking fees the kind of which you are speaking, is forbidden, although, as I said, it has been done by some mediums. Our seances here are run strictly on a donation basis. Whatever the person feels he is capable of giving, he will give."

I watched the man behind the desk. There are con men and there are con men. There are cheap carnival tricksters who stand outside wooden stalls that smell of elephant dung and human sweat and hand you a baseball as you walk by and say, hey lucky, knock over the milk bottles and win your pretty thing a teddy bear, just a quarter lucky, and lucky gives the man a quarter. There are genuine gypsy fortune-tellers whose Hungarian accents have a slight tinge of Lower East Side Manhattan.who can foresee a coming financial disaster and who will unselfishly offer to hold your life's savings until the danger has passed. There are psychics who for a slight fee that's really not so slight, will gladly give advice on when you should take a vacation, when you should get married, or whether or not that stock market investment you planned is a wise one. And then there are the con men who believe their own con and who are therefore not really con men at all. Whether the Reverend James Harnell had actually contacted Sheila Warren's dead brother by long-distance telephone or any other way was of little concern to me, although I had strong doubts. What mattered was that I was now convinced that he was convinced that he had.

"One more question, Reverend." I took the drawings of the diagrams out of my pocket and unfolded it on the desk in front of him. "Do those markings mean anything to you?"

He stared at the paper, turned it sideways, then right side up again. "No, I'm afraid not. What are they?"

"I was hoping you could tell me."

"Sorry. I suggest you take it to an expert on the occult. I'm afraid I'm not up on witchcraft and black magic and that sort of thing."

I took back the paper and gave him a business card. "If you think of anything else that might be of help, please give me a call."

"I'll do that."

We shook hands and I started for the door.

"Oh, Mr. Asch—"

I turned around.

"Feel free to stop by one of our Sunday services. We'd love to have you."

"Thanks. I'll try to make it sometime." The lie came easy.

I went through the front room, pausing momentarily to gaze at the PEACE and HARMONY cross on the wall. I listened. It was there, my father's voice, soft, saying, "We're all instruments of God's will, Jacob. Remember that, boy."

I listened again. The voice was gone. I opened the front door and went out to the street.

CHAPTER 5

Acid rock blared from the open doors of Isis and into the street, giving the passerby a little taste of what he would get inside. Once through the door, I found myself in a long, high-ceilinged room which was partitioned off into numerous carnival-like stalls. In the stalls, long-haired young men and women sat selling record albums and cheap stereo equipment, posters filled with weird distorted fluorescent shapes that squirmed to life when splashed with black light, water pipes, buckskin jackets, leather goods, candles shaped like twisted pieces of coral or driftwood or human phalluses. I asked the 300-pound bearded giant by the front door where I could find Sascha. He peered at me through a tiny pair of trip glasses that sat on the end of his nose, grunted, and pointed to the end of the room.

I found her standing behind a glass counter in which tarot cards, skin oils and various books on witchcraft and ceremonial magic were displayed, presumably for sale. She was wearing a loose-fitting, coarse sack dress and when she moved, I could tell she was bra-less. There was a good reason for it—I don't know if they make bras that big. She appeared to be in her late twenties and had long straggly hair which was the color of dead October leaves. Her eyes were pale green and harsh.

As I stepped up to the counter, I was hit hard by the stench of patchouli. Patchouli is an oil, and people who wear it tell me that it has strong attracting properties. That's what they tell me. To me, it brings to mind funeral processions and tombstones and the damp, rotten walls of the crypt.

She eyed me carefully for a few seconds before starting the pitch. "Would you like a reading?"

I tried to look dumb. "Huh?"

She turned on the mystery now, trying to look inscrutable. All part of the witch business, I guessed. She had cased her mark and was going after it. "Tarot card reading. The cards know all. They see all. They can tell you your past, present, and future."

"How much?"

"Five dollars."

I shrugged and dished out a five. What the hell, my expenses were covering it, and it's not every day you get a chance to learn about your past, present, *and* future for five bucks.

I sat down at a flimsy card table that was set up next to the counter. She sat down opposite me and pulled out a packet of cards. Then she opened the pack, skimmed through the deck and pulled out one, which she placed face-up on the table. It was a crowned figure seated on a throne, holding a sword in his hand.

"This is your Significator," she said. "It represents you. I've picked the King of Swords because Swords is the suit of dark hair and blue eyes. The King, because you are under forty."

She turned over another card and placed it directly on top of the King. It was another crowned figure holding a sword, this time seated between two pillars. The figure stared at me from its upside-down position.

"Justice reversed," she murmured. "Interesting. The main influence affecting your life right now is in the nature of law. You have a matter of law impending—perhaps a lawsuit—and you are concerned about it. Your Significator also has to do with justice and judgment. You have a powerful, discerning mind, and your judgments are harsh and final. You seem to have a deep concern with seeing justice done."

She wasn't bad, this witch.

She turned over another card and placed it across the other two. The man who looked at me upside-down was regal in appearance, seated on a low throne with a large cup in his hand. "This card shows the obstacles in your way at the present time," she said, looking up. "Beware of malice on the part of a man of position, possibly your employer. He is an evil man and before he is through he will try to do you much harm."

My employer . . . Ellman? No. A man of position. I was letting that one sink in when she turned up the next card and put it above the others. On it was a beautiful woman dressed in long, flowing robes. Her hair was a cluster of shiny stars and she was sitting on a pile of soft pillows. "Ah," she said, tapping the card gently with a forefinger, "The Empress. Your driving goal in life is the attainment of truth. You have an inquisitive mind that likes to piece things together. And since truth and justice go hand in hand, your ideals are lofty and noble, although at times uncompromising and inflexible."

"You've missed the most important part."

"What's that?"

"Where does it say anything in there about Sheila Warren?"

Her head jerked up, and her eyes narrowed. "I knew it. A goddamn cop." She started gathering up the cards on the table.

"Correction. Not cop. Private investigator."

"A pig's a pig, buster. Now get the hell out of here."

"I paid five bucks. You haven't finished my reading."

"I'm finished. Take it up with the Better Business Bureau. Now get out of here before I have you bounced."

42

"Tsk, tsk. Hostility will get you nowhere. Try to be a nicer person and I'll try to withhold the severity of my judgment. My judgment is harsh and final, remember? It's right there in the cards."

"Jimmy!" she called down to the end of the room.

The bearded giant looked up, then started to come over.

I wasn't worried. If worse came to worse, I figured I could always get a rock and a sling.

"This guy's hassling me, Jimmy."

"Out," the giant said, jerking a thumb back toward the door.

"Listen, Sascha, you've been lucky so far. I'm the only one that knows about your connection with Sheila Warren. But it could become common knowledge very quickly."

Goliath took a step forward and I took a step back, but not quickly enough. My arm disappeared in a huge hairy hand. I tried to wrench my arm free, but the grip just tightened. My arm started to get numb below the elbow.

"Out."

"You've got a limited vocabulary. Hands off, King Kong, unless you want to get slapped with an assault rap."

He smiled. "Assault? I was just defending myself. Everybody in the store seen it. You took a swing at me. You saw it didn't you, Sascha?"

"Yeah. He swung on you, all right. For no reason at all."

I thought about my choices. I could leave or I could stay and get broken into little pieces and even if by some miraculous turn of events I didn't get broken into little pieces, I doubted Sascha would answer questions. Some choices. "Okay, Sascha, you win. But you think about what I said."

I let Goliath march me out the door.

"Don't come back, buddy, or I'll kick your ass on the spot."

I walked down to the corner of the Boulevard. It was a

fine summer day in Hollywood. Hollywood in the daytime, stripped of its magical cloak of night and neon, is like a man in the advanced stages of syphilis who has been caught with his pants down. The male hustlers and fags and bulldykes and long-haired mooches bugging passersby for spare change were out in full force in the bright sunshine, treading sacrilegiously on the names of famous and not-so-famous show-business personalities that winked up at them from the star-studded sidewalk. On the corner, a group of tonsured and yellow-robed Hare Krishnas were swaying ecstatically to the rhythms they were beating out on their tomtoms and finger cymbals.

I stopped near them and one of them stepped out of the group and pushed a pamphlet at me. I refused it by holding up a hand, but he kept pushing it at me, smiling all the while as if he had just had a lobotomy and was liking it.

After a few minutes, I saw Sascha come out of Isis and cross the street and slip into a phone booth. I started across the street. The kid in the saffron robe kept pace with me, still trying to hand me the pamphlet, so I finally gave up and took it from him and he dropped back to join the group.

Sascha was just stepping out of the phone booth when I reached it. "I hope it was somebody interesting."

"You again? I thought I told you, creep, I've got nothing to say to you."

"I think you did, yes. But I'm bored and haven't got anything to do, so I figured I'd just kind of follow you around, in case you happened to change your mind."

She took a deep breath, her eyes rolling toward the sky. "All right, all right. What the hell do you want to know?"

"Let's go in here and talk," I said, motioning to the hamburger stand next to us on the sidewalk.

The stand was partially enclosed, the side facing the boulevard being open. The smell of greasy hamburgers cooking floated from behind the counter in front of which

44

miscellaneous vagrants stood waiting for time to pass with paper cups full of half-cold coffee. We slid into a small table by the glass wall.

"Coffee?"

She nodded. I got up and went to the counter, bringing back two cups. The coffee was foul. I figured that the obese, grease-spattered cook who had grudgingly poured it for me had probably boiled his socks in it just for spite. Sascha took a sip and grimaced. I knew better and just let the stuff sit there and turn slowly cold.

"Where were you the night of the murders, Sascha?"

"At an outdoor festival in Las Tunas Canyon. And I've got a dozen witnesses to back me up. Okay?"

"Okay. When did you first meet Mrs. Warren?"

"About a year ago. She wandered into the store one night. She was interested in occult books. I showed her a few. I gave her a reading. She was impressed. That was all."

"She come back after that?"

She took another sip of coffee and then began to pour in cream and sugar. "A few times. She consulted with me over a couple of problems."

"And that was all?"

"That was all."

"How many times would you say you saw her?"

"Two, three times."

"Ever go up to her house?"

"No."

I shook my head. "Sorry. No can buy. I know she attended at least one of your rituals. Her sister told me that. And you *were* up at the house."

"Who says so?"

"Her husband."

"That creep? That who you're working for? Figures. That bastard threatened me. Said he was going to have me arrested for fraud if I didn't stay away from his wife. Said

I was an unstabilizing influence on his wife's mind. That was a laugh. *He* was the unstabilizing influence if anybody was. But I fixed him."

"What do you mean, you 'fixed him'?"

"I put a curse on him. I made sure it was good and strong, too. It fixed him. He'll be convicted."

"Don't count your curses before they're hatched."

"And what's that supposed to mean?"

"Just that he might not have done it."

"It doesn't make any difference if he did or not. My curses never fail. He'll get it either way."

Who was I, one lowly private detective, to argue with the demonic forces of Hell?

"Getting back to Sheila Warren—"

"Okay, I was up at the house. I just don't want to get tied up with any murder investigation, that's all. Sheila called me up and asked me to come up and help her set up a private altar once, so I went up there."

"When was that?"

"About four months ago, I guess."

"That was the only time you were up there?"

"No. I was there one other time."

"Was Folsom there?"

"Yeah, I met him there. He wanted to film a documentary on witchcraft and asked if he could film one of my coven's rituals. I told him the meetings were strictly private, but that we could probably stage something for him. That's as far as it got."

"What did you think of Folsom?"

"He was all right."

"What did you think about Mrs. Warren?"

"She was a nice person. She had depth. We got along well. What do you want me to say?"

I took the drawing out of my pocket and showed it to her. "You know what this is?"

46

I thought I saw something register on her face, but it came and went so fast I couldn't be sure.

"No."

"The symbols are Egyptian."

"That's nice," she said, handing it back. "Look, I've got to get back to the store. I'm losing money sitting here. I've told you everything I know."

"I don't think you have, Sascha, but I think you've told me everything you're going to. You can go."

"Thanks loads."

I reached up and plucked a hair from my head, hoping silently it was a gray one, and handed it to her. "Here, you might need this. I hear curses work better if you have hair or fingernail parings or something like that."

She smiled. "Thanks. It'll save me a lot of trouble."

"Don't mention it. Always willing to help a witch in distress."

We left the restaurant. She turned right to go back to Isis and I turned left and headed down the Boulevard toward Cahuenga. The last time I had seen Murlock, the Archdruid of Los Angeles, I had still been working for the *Chronicle* and he had been giving yoga lessons and lectures on witchcraft in a rundown office building over by the La Brea Tar Pits. After doing some checking, I'd found he had opened a witchcraft museum on Cahuenga, just off Hollywood Boulevard.

The sign on the front of the dingy gray building was handpainted in yellow and orange letters. MAGICAL MYSTERY MUSEUM. There was only one way into the building and it opened onto a musty stairway that disappeared into darkness about five steps up. On the landing at the top of the stairs, I saw some light trickling through a crack in the dirty black curtains which hung down from the top of a doorway and I went in.

The room past the curtains was small and black. On

shelves around the walls were various labeled artifacts, goat's foot candles, ceremonial daggers, bottled powders of different colors. Besides the black-curtained door I had come through, there were two others just like it in the room, one straight ahead of me, and one to my right. Beside the one on my right was a small desk behind which a young hippie girl was standing, looking rather bored. In back of her, a sign said: SEE THE SECRETS OF MAGIC AND WITCHCRAFT—ADMISSION $1.

"One?" the girl asked.

"Where's Murlock?"

She motioned to the other doorway and I held my breath until I was safely through the dusty curtains and into the dark hallway beyond. The only door was at the end of the hall and it was closed. I turned the handle and went in without knocking.

The room was bare and the walls were gray-white and caked with dirt. Murlock was in one corner sitting on an empty orange crate. He was dressed in a black T-shirt and black levis and he was holding an acetylene torch in his right hand, aiming it at a small piece of silver metal he was holding with a pair of pliers in his left. A long-haired, lanky kid of sixteen or so was standing behind him, holding a straw basket full of little metal things like the one Murlock was working on. Roach clips.

I stood there silently for a few seconds, trying to figure out what it was about Murlock that was different. Then I saw it. The last time I had seen him he had hair.

He put the finishing touches on the roach clip, dipped it into a can of water by his side, squeezed off the knobs on the torch, and turned around. When he lifted his goggles, I noticed that he was also missing his eyebrows.

"Well, blessed be," he said. "My favorite intrepid reporter. What's new in the world of media?"

48

"I'm not a reporter anymore, Murlock. I'm now a private detective."

"Not really," he said, lifting a nonexistent eyebrow. "Just a second, Jake, and I'll be right with you,"

He turned to the kid, dropped the roach clip into the basket the kid was holding, and scowled. "Now get out there and don't come back until you've sold all of them."

The boy turned and was gone.

"The Archdruid of Los Angeles hawking roach clips on the Boulevard? Really."

He shrugged. "Things have been slow lately. I get a buck apiece for those things. Materials cost next to nothing and the labor's free. It all works out rather well."

I jerked my head toward the door. "One of your disciples?"

"The boy performs minor services in exchange for the privilege of basking in my radiant presence."

"Yes, I see. I barely recognized you with your shaved head."

"I had to shave it. The *prana*, you know."

"The what?"

"*Prana*, dear boy, *prana*. The serpent power of Kundalini. It radiates from me. My hair used to stand straight up from my head. I tried wearing hats for a while, but the force would just float them off my head. Bothersome, really."

"Yeah, I know how it is. My *prana* used to act up like that, too. Especially during electrical storms."

"Quite." He clapped his hands and rubbed the palms together. "Now, what is all this nonsense about being a private detective? What happened to the newspaper?"

"It's a long story. I got myself into a little jam and wound up blacklisted, so now I'm working as an investigator.

You're selling roach clips on Hollywood Boulevard and I'm peeping through keyholes."

He frowned as if he didn't want to be reminded of it. "Yes, such are the vagaries of existence, my friend. It is the Law of Karma. We are all paying for past sins. Now, to what do I owe a visit? I am receiving the message that you are not on a social call."

"You're right." I got out the drawing and handed it to him. "What is this?"

He studied it for a few seconds and then ran a hand over his bald head. "It's nothing, dear boy. Absolutely nothing."

"What do you mean?"

"It's nothing, that's what I mean. It is a child's doodling. It corresponds to nothing traditional in any occult discipline. It is a hodgepodge conglomeration made up by somebody who has been reading too much Dennis Wheatley fiction. The symbols inscribed around the circle are Egyptian, the one in the middle there is the symbol of Anubis, the jackal-headed lord of death. The double circle is a protective circle from goetic magic, designed to keep evil spirits out. But it is usually consecrated with the holy names of God to protect the operator. Here, it seems that whoever drew this abortion was intending to call in the demonic forces."

"Then you've never seen anything like it before?"

"There is so much of this junk floating around today. Everybody in the past few years has jumped head first into the occult boom and this is the inevitable result. Some kid reads a gothic novel and decides he's going to start a Satanic cult because it would be freaky. There is so much of this make-it-up-as-you-go-along stuff going down today, that it is quite impossible to keep up with it."

"Then you think that this was made up by somebody who didn't know what he was doing?"

"That is my expert opinion. Where did you get it?"

"From a friend. Somebody gave it to him and he asked me if I knew anybody who was an expert on the occult. I naturally thought of you."

"Naturally."

I put the paper away. "What do you know about a witch named Sascha who works at Isis?"

He tilted his head like a big, bald dog and looked at me with curiosity. "Stay away from that broad, my friend. She is definitely bad medicine."

"You know anything about her?"

"Only that she leans toward the demonic and that she's more of a bitch than a witch."

"Yeah, I know what you mean. I just got through talking with her. Anything else?"

He shrugged. "She has some rich clients."

"Know who?"

He shook his head. "No. But they drive some pretty fancy cars. Some nights I've seen limos pull up in front of Isis to pick her up."

"Well, look, thanks for your help," I said, opening the door. "And if one of your disciples just happens to be selling roach clips down around Isis some night and happens to spot a license number, I'd be really grateful. About ten roach clips' worth."

The dark eyes twinkled. "I will remember that, dear boy."

I handed him a card and he walked me down the hallway into the black room with the goat's foot candles. The young kid was leaning on the admission desk, talking to the girl as we walked in. His basket was still full.

Murlock lowered his head and glared. "I thought I told you not to come back until you sold all of them."

"I was just talking to Kathy."

51

"Get your ass out there and SELL! NOW!"

The kid hurriedly picked up the basket and ran for the stairs. By the time I hit the street, he was nowhere to be seen.

CHAPTER 6

June was definitely not a month for good beach weather, but today the fog was burning off exceptionally late, even for this time of year. I got off the freeway at Lincoln, went down to Claymoor Street and hung a right, and started cruising the neighborhood, looking for my number. The house was a stucco job, small and faded and pink. As with the rest of the houses on the block, it looked like fog and the corrosive salt air had taken its toll.

I parked in front and went up the cement walkway, past the long-gone lawn, and onto the small concrete porch. An old couch, its stuffing coming out of its tummy, sat on the porch by the front door staring at me malevolently. I knocked and the door opened a crack and an eye peeked out.

"Yes?"

"Mrs. Essen?"

"Yes?"

"I'd like to talk with you, if you don't mind."

"You a salesman or something?"

"No. I'm here to talk with you about your daughter."

Her eyes widened and her speech came in quick, panting gasps. "What about Rosemary? I haven't seen my daughter in two years. She doesn't live here anymore. She left home. What's she done? Are you a policeman?"

I couldn't think of which question to answer first, so I started with the last one. "Not exactly. I'm a private investigator."

I held up my identification and she looked right through it. "Is Rosemary in some sort of trouble?"

I took a deep breath and gave her my disarming smile. It helped loosen them up sometimes. "It's only incidentally regarding Rosemary, Mrs. Essen. I don't know if she's in any trouble or not. Can we talk inside?"

She opened the door reluctantly and stepped to one side. She was a tiny woman and in her oversized yellow house-dress, she looked as if she had been dehydrated and put into a container too large for her—like one of those cans of coffee in the market that you pick up and shake and hear the coffee rattling around inside. I don't know what could have shrunken her, but from looking at her face, my guess was despair. Streaks of gray ran through her otherwise mousy brown hair and her face was tired, reflecting years of strain that had eaten away the delicate sources of youth. She showed me to a couch in the living room and I sat down gladly. I was tired just looking at her. There was a brick fireplace to my right and from the top of it the face of a pretty young girl with long, blonde curls and large, soft brown eyes looked down at me.

She must have seen me looking at the picture, because she said: "That's my daughter. That's my Rosemary. But then I guess you already know that if you've come to talk about her, Mr.—You'll have to excuse me. I didn't even ask your name. You frightened me asking about Rosemary. I thought something was wrong."

I handed her a business card. She read it carefully, turned it over slowly in her hand and finally put it down on the coffee table in front of her as if it were made of glass and would break if she weren't careful. "Now what is it you want to talk with me about, Mr. Asch?"

"I'm working for an attorney who is defending John Meyer Warren. I'm trying to find out who murdered Mr. Warren's wife."

"You mean he didn't do it? The husband, I mean."

"That's what we're trying to find out."

Her mouth puckered into a tiny O, but nothing came out. After a few seconds, something did. "Well, whoever did it should get a medal. Not for the man's wife—I didn't mean that. But for that other trash—"

"Randy Folsom?"

She nodded, "You'll excuse the expression, mister, I don't usually use dirty language, but that man was a real bastard. I've never wished harm on anybody, but if anybody deserved to die, it was him."

"I'd like to hear about it."

"Why? What's it all got to do with the Warren fellow?"

"The police think that Folsom and Mrs. Warren were killed by her husband in a fit of jealous rage. If we can prove that she wasn't the objective of the killing, but Folsom was, well, you can see what it would do for our case."

"I see." She took a crumpled Kleenex out of her dress pocket, wiped her nose, and sat clutching the used tissue tightly in her hand.

"Rosemary met Folsom a few years ago at a party," she said. "When she was in high school she used to hang around with the fast kids, you know, and one of them—she never would tell me which one—took her to this party. She was sixteen then. It was one of those Hollywood freak parties—the kind you read about in those trashy magazines, thrown by those weird show-business degenerates. Anyway, this Folsom charmed Rosemary, like a snake would charm a bird—it must have been like that because Rosemary was a good girl. But all young girls are impressionable, you know how it is. And there are a lot of filthy animals like that Folsom just ready to prey on young, innocent girls."

She took a deep breath and let it out slowly. "After that party she kept on meeting him, without the permission of her father or me, of course. We never would have allowed such a thing, even if he wasn't who he was. We didn't allow Rosemary to date no older men. My husband worked hard all his life to raise Rosemary right, to teach her to do the right thing. He never would've let such a thing go on, if he would've known. But she kept on lying to us, saying that she was going out with her girl friends when she would really be meeting him."

"Did Rosemary tell you this?"

She nodded. "Later. After it all happened."

"Go on."

"Well, I don't know what he promised her, but he managed to seduce her. Actually, I do know what he told her. He promised her that she would be the star in his next movie. Can you imagine what that would do to a young, star-struck girl? It was true, what he told her, but the movie wasn't the kind she thought it was going to be. Folsom was making stag movies. Dirt and filth. That dirty animal seduced my daughter in front of his stinking cameras! How's that for disgusting? My poor Rosemary didn't even know she was being filmed. He showed it to her later and she came home that night screaming and crying and told us about it. That's when my husband called the police and they arrested him and his partner for statutory rape and contributing to the delinquency of a minor."

"Why were the charges dropped, Mrs. Essen?"

She began twisting the Kleenex she held in her hands. "When the police got to Folsom's place, they confiscated all his films, but the dirty ones weren't there. He'd taken them somewhere or destroyed them. I guess when he saw Rosemary all panicky he thought it'd be smart to get rid of them, and it *was* smart, because without the films, all the police had was Rosemary's testimony against his. The District Attorney told us that he doubted whether they could make the contributing charge stick."

"What about the statutory rape charge?"

The muscles in her face contracted into a painful grimace. "A lawyer came to see us right before the trial. He was representing Folsom. He said that if we took Folsom to court he'd drag Rosemary's name through the mud. He said that what had happened to her was bad enough, but that after he was through with her, after he got her on the stand, he'd tear her soul apart and we'd be lucky if we could piece her back together. He said he'd ask her detailed questions in front of the entire courtroom about what that filthy man did to her, how many times, how it felt, how did he do it, things like that. He said that if he were us he wouldn't want his daughter to suffer any more than she already had. He said it would be much wiser to drop the whole thing."

"And you agreed."

"Yes. My husband and I talked it over and we did."

There was something elusive in the way her eyes skirted mine and I decided to go after it. "How much did he offer you, Mrs. Essen?"

"Pardon me?"

"How much did he offer you to drop the charges?"

Her head jerked up and her eyes darted around the room, looking for an exit. When they did not find one, they settled back down to their customary dullness. Her shoulders went limp and she slumped back into the softness of the frayed couch. "My husband is a night watchman, Mr. Asch. Do you know what he makes a year? Do you know what two thousand dollars means to a family like ours? After we listened to that lawyer, Frank and I both decided it was the best thing to do. We thought Rosemary had been through enough."

"What did Rosemary think about the whole thing?"

"I don't know. She never said. After it all happened, she just would sit around the house, not saying anything to anybody. I think she felt we betrayed her somehow. We tried to explain things to her, how it was, but I guess she didn't understand. She ran away. I don't know, Mr. Asch, did we do the right thing?"

Emotional cripples like Mrs. Essen want one of two things when they ask a question like that—vindication or flagellation. She didn't strike me as the type who would want to be whipped for her sins.

"You did the only thing you could under the circumstances."

"You really think so?" She sounded hopeful, but I didn't want to elaborate and she wasn't sure enough of me to push it further.

"What about the other defendant, William Jeffries? What part did he play in the whole thing?"

"He was Folsom's photographer. The two of them were living together at the time in Hollywood, on Norling Drive. Rosemary said Jeffries was the one who filmed her in bed with Folsom. Later he made her go to bed with him too—forced her—while Folsom worked the camera. They did terrible things to her on that film. I just thank God it was destroyed."

"Do you know for sure it was destroyed?"

"It's gone anyway. I'm sure that's what they did with it after they found out Rosemary was going to make trouble for them. It was the only sensible thing for them to do."

"Do you have any idea where your daughter is now?"

"No. She's never written. Frank and I have been worried sick for two years, but there's nothing we can do."

"You could call Missing Persons."

"She's over age now. Besides, my husband is right. It wouldn't do any good—she wouldn't come home anyway."

She leaned across the coffee table.

"You know what the trouble with kids today is, Mr. Asch? They're ungrateful. They don't care how much you suffer trying to bring them up right, how much you sacrifice to feed them, sending them through school, trying to teach them the right thing to do. They think you owe it to them. . . ."

I put my pad away and stood, hoping to escape the rest of the speech. It was probably going to be the same one I'd heard a hundred times before from bewildered, guilt-ridden, hurt and angry parents, but I was half-tempted to stick around just to see if there would be any new touches added. When she saw I wasn't going to be the attentive, sympathetic audience she had hoped for, her voice trailed off and became still.

"I want to thank you for your help, Mrs. Essen."

She smiled weakly and stood with what seemed to be a great effort. "If you happen to run across Rosemary, Mr. Asch, give her our love."

I told her I would, knowing that there wasn't one chance in a million that I would run across her daughter in that city jungle out there, and left.

I strolled down the walk to the car, thinking about the remark Mrs. Essen had made about the snake-Folsom charming her bird-daughter, and about the superficial innocence that lay in those lush, soft brown eyes that occupied the privileged place on the living room mantel. I'd been half-tempted to tell Mrs. Essen that biologists had long since disclaimed any validity in the fable of bird-charming snakes, along with the myth that toads cause warts. Her daughter Rosemary had in all likelihood not been charmed by anybody. She had probably just been used to playing with rubber snakes for too long.

CHAPTER 7

After leaving Mrs. Essen, I went downtown to the Driver's Index Bureau and gave the clerk there Jeffries' name and date of birth and asked her to run an Alpha check on him and also to get an address. She came up with one car, a 1967 VW, license TIZ 451, and a current address of 804 Sherman Canal, Venice. I paid her four dollars for the info and left.

They tell me that the original architectural plans of Venice called for a network of canals on which brightly colored gondolas staffed with singing gondoliers were supposed to have floated. I don't know where the plans went awry, but all that floated in their brackish waters now were beer cans and milk cartons and occasional families of ducks who found the neighborhood easier pickings than some hostile marsh.

I crossed the cement arch that bridged Sherman Canal and parked on the other side. There were only four small, shabby houses on my side of the canal, and 804 was the third one. It was pea-green, except for big gray patches where the paint had flaked off its wooden sides in handfuls. The tiny front yard, which was surrounded by a ragged picket fence, was a dense, tangled cluster of century plants, yellow daisies and tall weeds.

I opened the gate and walked up the unpainted wooden steps to the porch and knocked on the screen door. Inside, I could hear the atonal wailings of a tenor sax. I waited.

In the canal in front of the house a male mallard was

pecking at a piece of milk carton that was bobbing lazily in the brown-black water while his mate paced back and forth on the shore, goading him on with her quacks. A few seconds passed. I knocked again.

Finally the inner door opened and through the screen, I could see a small, thin man dressed in jeans and a dirty T-shirt. His dark brown hair was long and oily and his eyes were small and black. We stood looking at each other for a few seconds, like two dumb animals.

"Mr. Jeffries?"

"What do you want?"

"I'm a private investigator. I'd like to talk to you about Randy Folsom."

I opened the screen door and showed him my I.D. He looked at it and then wheeled around suddenly. "Turn that fucking thing down!"

Somebody I couldn't see stuck a sponge in the sax.

"I haven't seen Randy in over a year."

"I'm flexible. How about Rosemary Essen? We can try that one."

"Beat it," he said, trying to close the door.

My hand was against it, holding it open. A little of the air from inside drifted out, teasing my nostrils with the strong, sweet smell of burning grass.

"Who is it, Bill?" called a female voice from inside somewhere. "Tell him to split."

"Look, I just want to ask you a few questions about Randy Folsom, that's all. It'll just take a few minutes."

"Listen, Mannix, I told you to split."

"You told me to beat it, *she* told me to split."

"Oh. A smart-ass."

"Could be. Why don't you get smart? It's not my business to lean on you, Jeffries. Don't make it my business."

"And what's that supposed to mean?"

"It means that I'm not interested in what kind of dope

61

you're smoking. Live and let live, that's what I always say. But I know some people downtown who don't have that attitude."

His teeth caught his lower lip and held it.

"It would really be a waste to have to flush all of that good grass down the toilet. Wise up. Don't buy yourself trouble. Talking to me will be a lot easier than talking to Narcotics."

He glanced at me mistrustfully and then the pressure on my hand released gradually and I knew I'd won the first battle. That only left the war for winning.

The living room, like the outside of the house, was pea-green. It was almost totally devoid of furniture, except for a couple of wicker chairs and a table with a lamp that looked like a piece of driftwood and the stereo components along the far wall. Different colored pillows were scattered around the scuffed wooden floor and against one of them lay a long-limbed blonde, sucking greedily on what was left of a joint. The temperature in the room must have been ninety degrees, the air close and humid. In one corner, an old radiator hissed at irregular, but frequent intervals.

Jeffries went over and flopped down next to the blonde. She was dressed in a gray granny dress that covered her body to the ankles, but judging from her neck and wrists, she looked quite thin. She was young and attractive, but had a used look, like a car dealer's demo model. I pulled up a yellow pillow and sat facing them cross-legged. Then I took off my coat and loosened my tie.

"Who's your friend?" the blonde asked.

"Go in the kitchen and make yourself useful. Go wash some dishes or something."

The girl ignored him and took another hit off the j.

"The goddamn dishes haven't been done since yesterday," he said, stronger this time.

She released a lungful of smoke in a noisy rush of air

and said, "I don't wanna wash the dishes."

"Then go in the fucking bedroom. Just split. I want to talk to the man alone."

Her long body stirred with great effort and she got up. She must have been a good three inches taller than his five-foot-five or six. "Jesus Christ, that's all you hadda say. Make such a fucking big thing out of everything."

He watched her leave, then turned to me. "How do I know you're really a private dick? How do I know you're not some Narc or something?"

"Quit playing games," I said. "If I was a Narc, I wouldn't have knocked. I would have hit that door so hard you wouldn't have had time to get up off the floor, and you know it."

He squinted and looked at me sideways. "So what do you want with me?"

"I told you. I want to ask you some questions about Randy Folsom."

"Why? What's your angle?"

"I'm trying to find out who killed him," I said. "The lawyer I'm working for is defending John Warren. He thinks his client is being railroaded for lack of available suspects."

"There shouldn't be any lack of suspects."

"Why do you say that?"

"Because Randy wasn't the most popular guy in the world."

"He had a lot of enemies?"

He smiled. "Let's just say he didn't have a lot of friends."

"How did you two get hooked up together?" I asked.

"I met Randy six years ago. I was filming documentaries for Ernest Teller. It was through Teller I met Randy. He was kind of hot then, Randy was, doing underground films. He was being built up as being another Andrew Simmons, except better. We worked together on a few things and became friends and then moved in together. After a while, Randy started to lose his touch, you know, reviews got pretty rough and the bread got thin. Then Randy started to lose confidence in himself. He started producing stags and asked me to stick around and help, and I did."

"What happened to Folsom the artist?"

"Shit, man, *you* start starving for awhile and see where your head goes."

I felt a twinge of empathy for Randy Folsom, wherever he was. I knew right where my head would go.

"When the money started to dry up, he needed a fast source of income and stags were it. It was after that that he started getting weird."

"Weird how?"

"I don't know how to put it into words, man, you know? The whole trip just blew his mind, and, uh, he just started getting far out. He got on a whole new trip, you know? Money. I stuck around for a while, because the bread *was* good, dig, but we lost the communication thing we had— you know?—and I finally couldn't take it any more and split."

"What did you two do with the stag films you made?"

"You mean what did Randy do with them. I just shot the things, that was all. It was Randy's gig. He paid me to shoot film and I shot it and that was that."

"Okay, what did he do with them?"

"Sold them to porno distributors. Except for the other ones."

"What other ones?"

"The ones we did for private parties."

"What kind of parties?"

"Some rich pervert would throw a party, right? He'd make a contact who would turn him on to Randy and so he'd hire Randy to come up and shoot the action. Some of those rich dudes are really freaks. S-M, lesbian scenes, the whole bit."

"And they'd pay to have themselves filmed."

He reached over and pulled a roach out of the baked-clay ashtray that was sitting on the floor beside him. Then he took out a cigarette and rolled it back and forth between his fingers. When all the tobacco was squeezed out of the paper tube, he dropped the roach into the half-empty cigarette, twisted the end of it together, stuck it in his mouth and lit it. Instant cocktail.

"Yeah, some of those cats really dug seeing themselves on film. Some guy who'd had a party the year before would throw another one and want a rerun, so he'd just get out the film of him balling so-and-so or the Duchess of Something-or-other balling the chauffeur. Some of these cats are really freaky. They've got plenty of bread so they got nothing better to do with their time than think of ways to be weird."

"And they'd pay Folsom for prints?"

He took a deep breath and held it, letting his voice out in a high-pitched squeak. "They'd buy prints and the negative—they'd want to make sure there weren't any loose copies floating around, dig? Except what they didn't know was Randy always made up two extra prints of every film he made and kept them. He said you never could tell when they might come in handy."

"What did he mean by that?"

"I don't know."

In none of the newspaper accounts of the murders was there mentioned any films being found, either at the Warren house or at Folsom's. Not that that fact was particularly unusual; certain police procedures aren't widely publicized. On a murder case, the investigating detectives often pick up what are known in police circles as "souvenirs," items which might be able to be used in some way to bring in information leading to the identity of the killers. The souvenir might be narcotics, vice information, anything that might be used to bribe, cajole, or even blackmail persons who might know something but are reluctant to spill it. Catching murderers is the only thing the boys down at Homicide are interested in and they aren't particular about whose toes they tread on to do it. What bothered me was that if the films Jeffries was talking about were in existence and found at the scene of the murder, why weren't the police making any use of them? If the films had been discovered, the police would have a larger list of suspects than Warren, but so far they weren't even admitting the possibility. And somehow I couldn't stretch Ellman's "guinea pig" theory that far.

"Do you remember any of the people whose parties you and Folsom filmed?"

"That was a long time ago. Four years. I didn't pay attention half the time. One cat I remember real well, though. A big producer. Had a house up in Coldwater. Chase Martin. That was a funny gig. A star was born that night."

"What do you mean?"

"Allison Shaw, the sex star of Empire Studios. Only her name wasn't Shaw then and she wasn't such hot stuff."

The name jarred me. Allison Shaw was hot stuff all right, the hottest item on the silver screen these days. "What's the story?"

"Randy used to supply girls sometimes for parties, for an extra fee, of course, and the Shaw chick—I don't remember what her real name is—used to do an occasional film for Randy. He met her when she was working as a cocktail waitress in some little joint off Western and they got kind of friendly. Anyway, one night this Martin dude calls Randy up and tells him that he wants him to film a party, right? but he says he needs some girls and Randy brings this Shaw

66

chick. Well, it winds up he leaves her there 'cause Martin digs her so much, and I could see it, you know, 'cause I mean she was a good-looking chick. Well, I just about croaked when I saw her starring in one of his pictures a year later. I didn't even know who Allison Shaw was 'cause of the name, right? and there was that face on the screen, whats-her-name Randy's chick doing her thing in a Chase Martin production. It really blew me out."

"How many people were at this party?"

"Half a dozen maybe. She was the only one that stood out in my mind though."

"What was Martin's bag?"

"Sadism. Whips and stuff like that. Bad trip. He played rough. That night—uh—he nearly took the back off one chick up there. They had to call a doctor up."

"You remember the doctor's name?"

"I don't even remember *your* name."

That I believed. "How many of these parties did you film with Folsom?"

"A few. Not many. Three, four, maybe."

"Not all of them were for Martin?"

"Only the one."

"You remember any of the others?"

"That was a long time ago. They were business people I'd never heard of. I only remember Martin because I'd seen a lot of his films and I knew who he was."

His lapses of memory were beginning to strain my credulity. "You don't remember any of the others?"

"Look, you said you wanted to know about Randy, so I'm telling you. What you buy is your own business. Randy handled all the business matters. Half the time he would just tell me, come on, we're going up to film a party tonight and I'd pack up my stuff and we'd split. He was close-lipped and half the time I didn't give a shit where we were going, so he didn't bother to tell me."

"And you didn't get any names?"

"Shit, man, are you hard of hearing or something?"

"Can you describe any of the people at these parties? You remember what any of them looked like?"

"Yeah, I remember. They all looked alike. You try shooting porno for a couple of years. After a while, all the people start to look alike. They don't even look real anymore; they look plastic. Big plastic dolls."

"How about the houses? You remember where you went to film?"

"Beverly Hills. The beach. Benedict Canyon. Big homes. And the fuckin' houses all looked alike, too. Big, plastic houses."

"You couldn't find any of them again if you had to?"

"I don't have to. But I couldn't find them again anyway."

I could see that more of the same questions would wind up in the same place; he either didn't remember or didn't want to talk about it. Either way, it wasn't going to help me any. "What about Rosemary Essen?"

He shrugged. "Randy was a fickle guy. Chicks dug him, but he didn't like having anything steady around. That was why it surprised me when I heard he'd shacked up with the Warren broad. But then she had bread—the bread could've had something to do with it. Anyway, this Rosemary, she got kind of hung up on Randy. He'd picked her up at some party and balled her and she kept coming around after that every day at all hours. He tripped out on her for a while 'cause she was young, and he liked 'em young, but after a while he got tired of her and told her to split. He didn't want her around anymore. Well, man, she flipped out. Started screaming that he was going to be sorry, that she was going to fix him good, shit like that. Randy got paranoid she was going to start trouble, so he ditched all his film, and it was a good thing he did or we'd be in the slams right now."

"A good thing for you. Bad for Randy."

He looked at me with confused, glassy eyes. "Huh?"

"Randy wouldn't be dead."

"Oh, yeah."

"Rosemary's mother told me her daughter said that you filmed Randy making it with her."

"That's a lot of bullshit. That chick was flipped out over Randy. She would've said anything to make trouble for him. That whole thing was a revenge trip. The D.A. saw that, too. That's why they dropped the contributing charge."

"She also told her mother that you forced her to make it with you."

"I never laid a goddamn hand on her."

"Then there was no film of her at all?"

"None. She knew Randy was making stags. She made up the film story to make trouble. That chick, as a matter of fact, was one reason Randy and I split up. Things were getting too hot and Randy was getting too loose. I didn't want to end up in the slams."

He took a final hit off the cocktail and mashed it out in the ashtray.

"You think Folsom might have planned to blackmail anybody with the extra films he'd made?"

"If he did, he wasn't letting me know about it. I don't know. Randy could've been into a lot of things since I saw him."

"How much money was he making then?"

"Plenty. But he never held on to anything. It all went through his fingers like water. That's why he was always looking for a soft touch, somebody who would like take care of him. And he found 'em, too. I don't know where, but he did. He had some rich fag friend who gave him money all the time, he's the one that got the lawyer that got the Essen chick off our back. Then I heard Randy was shacking up with the Warren broad."

"Did he say who this rich fag was?"

"Never told me and I never asked him."

Jeffries had to be one of the least curious people I'd ever met. He grew thoughtful for a minute, then looked up at me earnestly. "You know, I've been thinking and I think I know what Randy's problem was."

"What?"

"He might have gotten too kinky for his own good. That was another reason I had to like get away from him when I did. He was getting too far out for me. I think the money trip did it to him. You find yourself getting further and further out on a limb, right? and you look back and there's somebody sawing off the limb. I looked back one day and saw myself sawing it off. I knew it was time to get away from that whole scene."

I believed him. I believed he saw things. In all sorts of colors. I stood up and put my coat back on. "Well, thanks a lot for the information."

"I won't be called to testify or any of that bullshit, will I?"

"I doubt it."

"Good. Because my head's really not into that courtroom stuff, if you know what I mean."

Just then, his girlfriend came out of the other room and walked over to the ashtray and started poking through the ashes, looking for a roach.

"I thought I told you I wanted to talk to the man alone."

She continued to poke. "He's leaving, ain't he?"

"You were listening to the whole thing from the bedroom, weren't you?"

"So what if I was?"

They were shouting obscenities at one another as I opened the door and stepped out on the porch. After the stuffy, grass-filled heat of the room, the moist sea air felt cool and refreshing against my cheek. I went down the walkway and opened the front gate. The mallards in the canal were still pecking away at the garbage, quacking up a storm.

"You guys think you got troubles," I said, and walked along the canal, back toward the car.

CHAPTER 8

If judged on the sheer force of personality, Chase Martin would probably have been sentenced by a jury of his movie-making peers to be drawn, quartered, shot, and hung in front of a meeting of the Academy of Motion Picture Arts and Sciences. He had an unmatched reputation for ruth-lessness. He dealt in human lives, judging and executing, making—and just as fast breaking—stars from talents and no-talents. And even the ones he had made expressed no particular love of the man, no real feeling of gratitude, but rather an instinctive sense of caution.

Although his work had been consistently blasted by crit-ics as being banal and exploitative, even those who hated him—which was almost anybody at all—had to admit that Chase Martin was an administrative genius. Forceful and intelligent, he possessed an uncanny ability for making all the right moves, for converting other people's strengths and weaknesses into cold, hard cash. When Empire Studios was under the gun, facing possible bankruptcy, President Saul Halpern called an emergency meeting of the board and put forth the suggestion that they offer a million-dollar contract and complete run of the studio to entice Martin from the embrace of Allied International. They did, he came, and in a little over two years, Empire was back operat-ing in the black.

Chase Martin was a very important man and certainly not the most accessible. His secretary was not about to put me through to him until I told her it was about a film he had financed several years ago and that it was urgent. When she asked my name, I told her to tell him it was Randy Folsom.

"Who the hell is this?" the voice snapped sharply into the line.

"My name is Jacob Asch, Mr. Martin. I'm a private investigator. I'd like to talk to you about Randy Folsom."

"I don't know any Randy Folsom."

"I'm very sorry. I must have the wrong Chase Martin. I'm looking for the Chase Martin who hired Randy Folsom three years ago to film certain extracurricular activities up at his house in Coldwater Canyon. Good-bye."

"Wait a minute."

"Yeah?"

"Be here at the studios tonight at nine," he said and hung up.

The security guard, a thin, gray little man dressed in a darker gray uniform, stepped out of his kiosk and held up a wrinkled hand.

"Jacob Asch to see Mr. Martin."

He ran a bony finger down his roster. "Okay. Swing your car around and park it anywhere over there," he said, pointing toward a long, low, wooden building that looked like an army barracks. "Mr. Martin's office is in that building there. Second door on your left as you go in."

I thanked him and parked. I went up the outside steps and down the long hallway until I found the door marked *Chase Martin, Executive Producer.* My knock was answered by a tall blond man with pale eyes.

"Mr. Martin's expecting me."

"What's the name?"

"Asch."

He opened the door and took two steps back and waved me in. The reception room was small. Aside from the standard office fare, the only furniture in the room was a long settee that lined the wall by the front door. On that, a man who had a football helmet for a head and a nose that looked as if it might have been broken three or four times, sat disinterestedly reading a magazine.

"Lift the arms," the blond man said.

I lifted the arms. He gave me a quick frisk, came out with my wallet, and motioned me toward another door. He knocked, opened it, and pushed me through.

The office I was pushed into was something. The walls were a deep burgundy color, the carpeting, the draperies, and the leather furniture, all being cream. The main source of decoration in the room were photographs of Chase Martin in friendly poses with various famous personalities, show business and political. In front of the windows was a large, drawerless, glass desk, and behind the desk was Chase Martin.

He was heavy and had a thick neck on which rested a wide, red face. His hair was gray and his eyes were large and blue and watery. He was wearing a navy sports jacket and a pink-striped shirt open at the neck.

There was a riding crop in his hand, and he was tapping it gently on the desk as I walked in. He looked at me as if I were a blood-rare steak he had ordered well done and had already sent back twice. He didn't bother with the formality of shaking hands, so I didn't bother with the formality of waiting to be asked to sit down.

The blond man walked over to the desk and handed Martin my wallet.

"I'll buzz if I need you. Stay close."

The blond man nodded and left, closing the door behind him. Martin looked through my wallet, then tossed it at me. I caught it before it hit me in the face. I could tell I was going to love him.

"What's all the muscle for?"

"Get cute and you'll find out what it's for."

"You misunderstand me, Mr. Martin. I'm a businessman. I'm not here for any rough stuff. I'm just here to sell a piece of film, and that's all I'm here for."

"What film is that?"

"A print of a film of a party that Randy Folsom shot up at your Coldwater Canyon home a few years back."

"I don't know what you're talking about."

"Then why did you tell me to come over tonight? Let's cut the bullshit. You and I both know that your biggest box office draw could go down the tubes very quickly if that film ever got released for public consumption. And the editor of *Screen Delight* would give his right arm for an exclusive."

"And just who would that be?"

"Allison Shaw?"

"I still don't know what you're talking about."

"Sorry to have wasted your time then. I guess I'll stop by *Screen Delight* and check out the market." I got up and started for the door.

"Wait—"

I stopped.

"How much?"

"I figure it would be worth at least $25,000 to you to protect your reputation and the reputation of your biggest star."

"That's ridiculous."

"Not really. Allison Shaw makes ten times that much for one picture. And remember—if she goes, you go. So actually, you're getting double your money's worth."

"How did you happen to get this film?"

"That's my business."

"I'm making it my business."

"Please, Mr. Martin, don't get tough. What are you going to do, hit me with your riding crop there? Or whip me with a cat-o'-nine-tails? I'm not one of your up-and-coming starlets. You might find you'd have a little harder time of it."

He looked angry, and he was trying his best to contain it. "How do I know you have the print?"

"I'll bring you in a sample film clip tomorrow. Then we can make the necessary arrangements."

He leaned forward, putting all his weight on the two red hands on the glass desk. "Now you listen, and you listen good, punk—I'll make YOU an offer. In about thirty seconds you're going to take a ride with those two boys out there. You're going to go get that film and you're going to bring it back here to me. For that I will pay you $5,000 and let you keep both your legs and both your arms."

I shook my head. "No good. If you were the only market, your threats would probably carry more weight. Look— $25,000 is a fair price. *Screen Delight* would pay at least that for the film and you know it. I'm actually giving you a break. You have me worked over and you'd be forcing me to sell it to them."

He looked like he had just taken a bite out of a nice, juicy lemon. His knuckles were white around the riding crop. "All right, goddamn it. You bring in the clip tomorrow and we'll deal. Now get out. You're starting to stink up my office."

I didn't move.

He reached over and poised a finger above the intercom button. "I'm going to count to three and if your ass isn't out that door, I'm going to buzz the outer office and have it kicked out. One—"

"Buzz away, if you can afford the publicity of being sucked right into the middle of a murder investigation. Ah, I can see the headlines now. PRODUCER AND STAR LINKED TO BRUTAL SOCIALITE SLAYINGS. Beautiful copy."

Two never came. "Murder? What the hell are you talking about?"

"I'm no blackmailer, Mr. Martin. I'm working for John

Warren's attorney, investigating the murders of Warren's wife and Folsom. I told you I had that print and wanted to sell it because it was the sure way I could get in to see you. Also, I wanted to see how you'd react to blackmail."

"Why?"

"Because I found out about Folsom's illustrious career as a movie producer and I also found out that he had made extra prints of all the little parties like yours he'd filmed. I guessed that he was using them for blackmail purposes. You just proved it to me."

"Yeah? How?"

"If Folsom hadn't approached you, you wouldn't have any reason to believe that any extra prints existed. Twenty-five G's shows a pretty strong belief."

"So what's all that got to do with Warren killing his wife?"

"I don't think Warren murdered his wife. I think whoever did it did it to get those films back."

He sneered. "You're treading on thin ice coming around here making the kind of suggestions you're making—"

"I'm not making any suggestions. I'm just saying that so far your name has stayed out of the papers. If you want to keep it out, you might answer a few questions for me."

He didn't say anything. He just stared and tapped the riding crop against his palm.

"We're not going to have to play the whole game again, are we—the one where I stand up and start to leave, and you call me back? It's been a long day, Mr. Martin, and I'm tired. Have a heart. Save me a trip to the door."

"How would you like to go to work for Empire, Asch? I can tell you'd be a hell of a PR man. I could start you at a salary of—say, eight hundred a week?"

"I don't want a job, just some answers. Folsom did try to put the bite on you, didn't he?"

He looked like he was thinking it over. "Yes. He came

here to the studios about a week before he was murdered. He contacted Allison and told her about the extra print and said he wanted ten thousand for it. She told me and after talking it over, we decided to pay it. She made the appointment for the payoff, but he never showed up. The next thing we knew, he was dead."

"How did she take that?"

"How the hell was she going to take it? She was upset. That print could ruin both of us. After Folsom was killed, we had no idea what had happened to it. Allison has been a nervous wreck. She breaks out into a cold sweat every time she picks up a copy of *Screen Delight*, half-expecting to see her picture on the cover."

"I'd like to talk to her. Where can I get in touch with her?"

"She's night shooting tonight over on Lot C."

"You think you could arrange for me to talk with her?"

"What for? I can tell you everything she can. There's no need to bother her."

"Maybe not, but I'd still like to talk to her."

"You're a stubborn boy, aren't you? Listen, Asch, you don't really think either of us had anything to do with those murders, do you?"

"I don't think anything at this point. I'm just trying to sift through the facts."

"Look, if I killed Folsom to get that film back, I wouldn't have been willing to pay you twenty-five grand for it, would I?"

"If what you say is true, you've got nothing to worry about. And the more cooperation you show me, the quicker I'll be able to prove it. Now, how about Miss Shaw?"

"I'll take you over there myself, just to show you how cooperative I can be."

We went into the reception room and the two dead-end

kids started to get up, but Martin waved them down. "We're going over to Lot C. Stay here. I'll be back in twenty minutes or so."

Outside, we hopped into an electric golf cart that stood by the door and skimmed down the dark and deserted streets of a western town. The moon shone over the tops of the buildings, throwing eerie shadows across our path. The night lent the set an aura of unreality and I felt uncomfortably like an intruder clumsily invading the privacy of somebody's long-forgotten dream. The silence of the dream soaked into my skin and I shuddered.

We went on through the town, past a half dozen medieval siege machines, and around the plywood back of a castle plinth. The top of the castle battlements were bathed in a halo of light, and when we rounded the edge of the structure, I saw the source of the halo. Under blazing floodlights, bulldozers and dump trucks were clearing away what was left of a city. The job was over half-done, only a few buildings left standing over piles of rubble, so it was impossible to tell whether it had been London, Paris, New York, or Winnemucca, Nevada. I looked over at Martin. He had stopped the cart and was watching the scene, a distant look in his eyes.

"Beautiful, isn't it?"

I looked again. A bulldozer was moving on a section of storefront, converting it into another pile of rubble. I wondered if we were looking at the same thing.

"The head of a studio exercises a sort of godly power, Asch. He can turn his wildest fantasies into reality. He can reproduce the cities of the world in the minutest detail, and then, with a wave of a hand, order them destroyed."

It was nice to know I was in the company of a god; it made me feel secure. He sat watching for a few seconds more, then jerked the cart into motion. We zipped down a narrow alleyway that ran between two huge, hangarlike sound stages, rounded a corner, and once again I was dazzled by the glare of lights.

We were in front of another city set, this one a grimy downtown street lined with sleazy bars and cheap all-night cafes. There were no bulldozers this time. Allison Shaw was standing in front of one of the bars, surrounded by hot lights and camera dollies and sound booms. She was dressed in a long, beige camel hair coat and a dark-brown hat with a wide floppy brim. She looked just as I had seen her in her pictures, except she was taller than I thought she'd be. She had fine, high cheekbones, large, dark eyes and a wide, proud mouth. The coat covered her million-dollar body and her long blonde hair was pulled up and tucked away somewhere underneath the hat. She was beautiful all right, but it was a stony, sculpted beauty that radiated little warmth. What she was selling on the screen was fast and impersonal, and it showed. She was the type every man would want to run away with—for a weekend.

Martin walked over and said something to the director, who then turned around and clapped his hands and yelled to the camera crew: "Okay, that's it for tonight. Let's wind it up."

Martin came back to the cart and hopped in. "We'll meet her at her dressing room."

We drove back down the alleyway and parked outside one of the hangars. I followed Martin through the huge sliding door. The sound stage was dark and empty and our footsteps were insignificant and lonely inside. We went down a hallway and stopped in front of a row of temporary-looking plywood dressing rooms. After a couple of minutes, I heard footsteps and Allison Shaw came up. She looked at Martin and then gazed searchingly at me.

"What do you want, Chase?" Her voice was decidedly hostile.

"This gentleman is a detective. Mr. Asch, Miss Shaw. He'd like to talk to you."

"What about?"

"I'll let him explain inside."

The three of us adjourned up the steps and into the dressing room. The inside was not as bad as the outside. It looked comfortable and was big enough to house a bed, a low vanity table with a large mirrored back, its edges studded with light bulbs, and a couple of chairs. There was a bathroom to the left and a walk-in closet to the right. On the dressing table were large jars and small jars and medium-sized jars, all filled with liquid beauty and beauty remover.

"Welcome to the dump," she said. "Make yourself at home."

In the room at close range, her face had an orange cast to it. The makeup, I figured. She threw a disdainful look at Martin. "I'm not usually such a lousy hostess, Mr. Asch. It's my surroundings. If Mr. Cheapskate over there would get his builders off their asses and on those new dressing rooms we were all promised five months ago, I'd be able to do better."

Martin didn't say anything, but just sat there smiling.

"If you'll excuse me for a minute," she said and disappeared into the bathroom. When she came out, she was dressed in a white terrycloth bathrobe. Martin's smile had turned to plaster and looked ludicrous hanging on his face.

She sat down in front of the mirror, pulled a pint of scotch from the dressing table drawer, and poured herself a drink.

"Care for some? Scotch is all I have." She said it to nobody in particular and she didn't seem to mind when nobody in particular answered.

She put the glass down and opened a jar of cold cream and began removing the orange makeup. The silence that blanketed the room was a respectful silence, like the quiet that stands guard over a funeral. We were witnessing the death of a star. After she had finished, she turned toward me. The harsh lights in the room were not kind to her face, marking dark circles under her eyes and tiny lines at their edges, the results of too many seconal nights and amphetamine mornings. When she turned at a certain angle, I noticed that her long honey-blonde hair had short, dark roots. "Now what's this all about?"

"Mr. Asch is trying to find out who killed Randy Folsom, and he thought we might have some knowledge of the matter."

She aged five years in front of my eyes. "Why would he think that?"

"Because he knows about the film."

She banged her glass down on the table after taking a good gulp. "Jesus Christ! Everybody in the fucking world knows about that film. Why the hell don't we just send out a bulletin and some sample film clips to *Screen Delight*?" A wry smile spread on her face. "It's ironic, isn't it, Mr. Asch, that the same film that launched me into fame and fortune is threatening to yank me out again? Now that's poetic justice!"

"Calm down, Allison," Martin said, trying to sound soothing. His kind of soothing was like salt in an open wound.

"The Lord giveth and the Lord taketh away, eh, Chase?"

"Let's not get melodramatic."

She turned to me. "If you're looking for whoever it was who murdered Randy Folsom, you'll have to look somewhere else. He tried to blackmail me for what was on that film, yes, but I didn't kill him. And I've got witnesses to prove it. Where were you that night, Chase? I don't think I ever asked you."

"You know I was at Madylyn Aronson's party. Don't get funny."

She laughed. It was deep and throaty. "I just thought Mr. Asch might like to know. I'd check it out with Madylyn if I were you, Mr. Asch. Chase here is a violent man—unpredictably violent."

"Now look here, Allison—"

"No, YOU look here, you fat sadist, get the hell out of my dressing room!"

She was a woman of many moods, all of them being constantly shuffled around so that you never knew which one was going to come up next.

Martin stood up and pointed a finger at her. "You watch your mouth in front of strangers, Allison. I'm warning you. I think that you forget sometimes where you came from and that you can be put back there just as easily."

"By you? Go ahead and break my contract. Elliott McGiver was over just last week. You know Elliott, don't you, dear? He'd be delighted to hear the news that you've decided to sever our business relationship. Why don't you call him?"

Martin turned to me. "I don't think the three of us are going to accomplish very much together, so I'll leave you two alone."

He stalked out and I listened to his footsteps going down the stairs. "I think you made him mad."

She poured herself another slug of scotch and downed it. "That sow's ear. What can he do to me now? Nothing, that's what. He created a Frankenstein." She chuckled. "That's what I am—a goddamn Frankenstein."

"He's a charming man."

"Mister, you don't know the half of it."

"You seemed to be implying that he might have had something to do with the murders."

"I was just trying to get him pissed off."

"Do you think he'd be capable of murder?"

"Capable?" She pulled down the shoulder of the robe, exposing three parallel lines of shiny white tissue each about three inches long. "See that? That's how nice that perverted bastard is. Every time I show my back in public now I've got to use makeup because of that fat pig. He's a real charmer, all right."

She tilted back her head and knocked down the scotch that remained in the glass. "What's your line? You've heard of that program, haven't you?"

She seemed to be getting slightly drunk, which was all right by me. Drink is good for confession and confession is good for the soul. "That depends."

"On what?"

"On what I'm hired to do."

"So what did Chase hire you to do? And why did he send you in to see me?"

"I'm not working for Martin. And he didn't send me. I sort of insisted on seeing you."

She didn't look impressed. "About Randy Folsom."

"That's right."

"I abandoned Christian charity a long time ago. The returns on my investment were too low. What's in it for me?"

"Your name stays out of the papers."

She sat thoughtfully for a few seconds, tapping her long fingernails on the dressing table. Finally, she leaned back. "Okay, Mr. Asch, what do you want to know?"

"For starters, I'd like to know who you were with the night of the murders."

She laughed again. She laughed quite a bit. "Mister, you've really got a lot of tact." She scribbled something down on a piece of paper and handed it to me. It said: Jerry and Margaret Taylor. 1211 South Alton Way, Beverly Hills.

"We were eating late at the Moonlighter's Inn, discussing work on a new film."

I folded the paper and put it in my pocket. "When did Folsom contact you about the extra print?"

"A few days before he was killed. But he never showed up to collect."

"Don't you think that was kind of strange?"

"Look, you're talking to a biased witness. I think the whole goddamn thing was strange. I've been a basket case ever since it happened. Maybe you don't realize it, but my whole career is at stake here. It could go down the drain like that—" Her fingers snapped loudly, a sharp *click*.

"And you've gotten kind of used to being a star."

"Goddamn straight, mister. You see this beautiful blonde hair? Well, it's not really blonde. Underneath all that dye somewhere is black. You know what my real name is? It's not Shaw. It's Olvera." She spat the name out as if she were ashamed to have it in her mouth. "I started working as a waitress in a grubby, roach-infested restaurant in East L.A. when I was thirteen. I paid to make it out of that shit, with scars administered by fat, slimy animals like Chase Martin, and I'm not about to give back the fare. I made it out and I'm staying out and nobody's going to put me back in."

What glamour had been left after the removal of the makeup was flaking off now, layer by layer. We glared at each other. "You sound like you'd kill to stay out."

"I probably would. But I didn't kill Randy Folsom."

"You knew Folsom before you went up to Martin's party, is that right?"

"Let's not play cat and mouse, huh? You already know I knew him or you wouldn't be asking me."

"I got one story. I'd like to see if yours matches it."

She stared pensively into the scotch that lay in the bottom of her glass. She opened a drawer and pulled out a

85

pack of cigarettes. Her fingers dug around inside the cellophane package until she came up with one. I took out a book of matches I always carry around for such occasions and lit it for her. "Okay," she said, "let's tell it. Why the hell not? You probably know it all anyway." She waved the fingers holding the cigarette around at the walls of the dressing room. "This is a sordid business, mister, and most of the 'beautiful' people in it come from sordid backgrounds. It's a business for pimps and whores, and before you get anywhere in it, you put out plenty."

Preamble. They always give a preamble before they start, like a pitcher going into his wind-up. She was about to pitch.

"I was working cocktails in a club downtown called the Bird's Nest. Randy used to come in a couple of times a week and sit around and drink and pretty soon we got friendly. He asked me if I'd like to pick up some spare cash. I asked how, and he told me by acting in a film he was making. The money he offered was good and I was turning a couple of tricks a week on the side anyway, so I said okay. After that, I did a couple more things for him and then one night he calls me up and tells me he had a gig to do at a private party in Beverly Hills and he thought it could be a good break for me because the guy who was throwing the party was a big producer. It was Chase's party. From the minute I got there Chase saw my potential. He arranged for a screen test the next day and a few days later I signed a contract for Empire. So there it is—my success story—considerably shortened and cleaned up for public consumption, but that's the core of it. Small-time whore becomes big-time star. Like it?"

I didn't particularly like it. We're all whores in one way or another; it's a fact of life. It just depends on how badly we want what we want and what we're willing to sell to get it. I learned that the hard way.

She poured herself another drink.

"Don't you think you've had enough of that?"

She gave me a sly look. "You only say that because you're sober. If you were drinking, you wouldn't think so. Have a drink."

"No thanks."

"C'mon. I don't like to drink alone."

Her drinking was like the rest of her life—high speed. But she was moving at high speed toward the edge of a cliff and was going too fast to stop. She saw it coming—I could see it in her eyes—and she saw that I saw. That was probably why she wanted me on board for company.

"No thanks."

She shrugged and sighed, and slumped back in her chair.

"Why didn't you call the police after Folsom came to see you?"

"Now *that* is a stupid question. Nothing is going to put me back in the rat race I was in. If I could've bought him off for fifty grand I would've done it. I've got another studio on the hook that wants to buy my contract for half a million dollars. *Half a million.* Randy was a cheapie."

"Who else was at the party that night at Martin's?"

"Let's see—there was Bill Drake, Mary Ellen Lewis, Curt Wallenberg, Phyllis Harriman. And some little dark-haired girl Chase picked up somewhere."

"You know where I can find them?"

"Chase can tell you where to find Drake. But I don't think he'd be a hot suspect."

"Why not?"

"He was injured in a car accident about a year ago. Unless your murderer did the job in a wheelchair, it wasn't Drake." She laughed for some obscure reason.

"And the rest?"

She looked into her glass. It was empty. Then she looked at the bottle. It was also empty. She shrugged in disappointment and tightened the belt of the robe. "Curt's in the south of France filming. He's one of Chase's directors. Mary Ellen Lewis, the last time I heard, had a supporting role in an off-Broadway musical I don't remember the name of. Phyllis you can find at Forest Lawn. She o.d.'d on Tuinals about three months ago. Too bad, too. She was the only one of the whole bunch I'd give you two cents for."

"Did you ever do any other parties for Folsom?"

"No. The other stuff I shot for him was straight blue."

"And he never mentioned any names of anybody whose parties he'd filmed?"

"Not to me. We weren't that intimate."

"What about the little dark-haired girl you mentioned?"

"The hippie? She was young. Chase picked her up hitch-hiking on the Strip and offered her fifty bucks to come up to the house. He wound up paying her a lot more than that to keep her mouth shut."

"What happened?"

"He used a whip on her. Beat her so bad that she passed out from the pain. She was screaming for him to stop, but he kept right on. Her back was a real mess. They got a doctor up there to patch her up."

"What happened to her?"

"Curt drove her down to the Strip. That's where she said she wanted to go. Said she had friends there. When I saw that little episode, believe me, I thought twice about what I was getting into. Chase had already promised me a screen test, but after I saw him work that little girl over, I thought to myself, to hell with it, to hell with the screen test, these people are nuts."

"But you stuck with it."

"Yeah, I stuck with it."

I sat looking at her, wondering what was going to happen to her in a few years when the offers for starring roles stopped coming in, when the bags under her eyes got too big to hide with makeup and her breasts started to sag and the skin began to hang loose underneath her chin. She didn't strike me as the type to age gracefully. The ones that clung that desperately seldom do. I actually felt kind of sorry for her.

"You interested in the occult, Miss Shaw?"

"Me? No. It's all a bunch of crap to me. Why?"

"I've just sort of acquired a deep interest in the subject."

"In that case, you should get together with Chase. He's nutty about that sort of thing. Has his own astrologer on the payroll and won't make a move without him. Around here, if Mars isn't in the house of Venus, the cameras don't roll."

She looked at me through half-closed, weighted lids. "Say, Asch, what are you going to do with that film if you happen to run across it somewhere?"

"That depends on what's on it. Who knows? I might give it to you as a present."

"Don't do that. Make Chase pay for it. I'm sure he'd give you a good price. You look like you could use the money. And I love to see Chase pay for things. It gives me a deep satisfaction that's hard to put into words."

"The Lord giveth and the Lord taketh away," I said, standing up. "Goodbye, Miss Shaw. It's been nice."

She was smiling as I closed the door, but I wasn't sure if she saw me. Martin was waiting at the cart.

"Did you two have an educational chat?"

"Very. How can I get in touch with Bill Drake?"

He eyed me curiously. "He's listed. Lives on Ames Drive in Long Beach. Why do you want to talk to Bill?"

"No particular reason. By the way, do you want to give me Madylyn Aronson's number or should I go to a lot of trouble to dig it up?"

"No need. It's 274–1211. You aren't a very trusting soul, are you, Asch?"

"If I was, I wouldn't be in the business I'm in. Why—are you a trusting soul?"

He smiled. "If I was, I wouldn't be in the business I'm in."

We made the rest of the trip back to the parking lot in silence, and when we finally jolted to a stop, Martin put his fingers on the sleeve of my coat. "If you do recover those films, do remember me. Like I said before, I could make it worth your while."

He had better sense than to offer his hand. When he reached the door of the barracks, he turned around. "Give my regards to Madylyn."

"I'll do that."

I walked across the lot feeling in dire need of a shower.

CHAPTER 9

It was ten past eleven and I was tired. For the last half hour, my eyes had been glued to the string of red brake lights that stretched out to infinity in front of me as I inched my way home. At the Sepulveda exit, I passed what had backed up traffic for ten miles. It was a red Datsun which had apparently been going north on the freeway, run through the center divider fence, and finally come to rest on its top in the middle of the southbound lanes.

A towtruck was just hooking up to the car's front bumper now and although the ambulance had come and gone ten minutes ago, gawkers still crept slowly by the crinkled car, ignoring the highway patrolmen's frustrated hands waving them on in the pink flare light.

I got off on Century Boulevard East, drove down to Bufort Street and made a right. The house I lived in was at the end of the block, a yellow, flat-topped, stucco box with terra-cotta tiles running across the edge of the roof. The windows were smaller than I would have liked and the furniture could only be described as Early Austere, but it had a fireplace and the carpeting had only a couple of holes in it. The rent was only $80 a month, which was why I had moved in in the first place.

The house was chopped up into two sections. I rented the front half. Since the Sandovals had moved out two months ago with their four kids, mumbling something about *el ruido*, the noise, the back half had been vacant. Actually, they had lasted a pretty long time—four months

—but I still held the record at nine. The reason they had left was the same reason everybody left and the same reason that the rent was so cheap—the house lay directly in the approach pattern of L.A. International Airport. But at eighty bucks a month, my *ruido* threshold had quite a way to go before it reached the intolerable level.

Bufort Street is a narrow street and the big silver Rolls that sat in front of my house took up about half its width. I squeezed by on the right and swung into my gravel driveway and parked. As I got out and locked my car, the door of the Rolls opened and Gloria Pilsen stepped out. She came up the driveway. She was wearing a stark-white jumpsuit and white shoes and a gold necklace that didn't look like it cost more than two or three grand. Her hair was pulled back and tied, and either that or the dim light in the driveway made her look younger than she had at her house.

"Hello, Jake darling. You certainly do keep late hours."

"How long have you been waiting here?"

"Scads of ages. Half an hour at least."

"What have you got there?" I asked, pointing to the brown paper bag under her arm.

"Just a bottle of Chivas Regal. I made some inquiries and found out you don't drink scotch and I absolutely detest bourbon, so I brought my own along. I hope it doesn't offend you. What is that godawful smell?"

"Jet fuel. It smells like that all the time around here. L.A. International is about a quarter of a mile that way. How did you find out where I lived?"

"The same way I found out you drink bourbon. But we can talk about that inside, can't we? You *are* going to invite me in?"

"If you're going to come in, you'd better lock up that big, beautiful car. Otherwise, you might not have any seats in it when you come back out."

"I didn't realize it was *that* kind of a neighborhood."

"Now you realize."

She handed me the paper bag with the Chivas Regal and I went to the front door and unlocked it. There was a note tacked to the door from Mr. Gutierrez, my landlord, asking me to call him tonight when I got in, no matter how late. I took the note inside and went into the kitchen and opened the cupboard. I started to reach for the Early Times, then said to hell with it, if she can drink Chivas Regal, I can drink Wild Turkey, and grabbed the good stuff. The drinks had already been made, and I was in an easy chair sipping mine by the time she came in.

"Water all right?"

"Fine." She took the glass and sipped. "You make a good drink."

"I'm glad it's okay."

"So how's the big investigation going?"

"All right."

"All right? You mean you haven't proved that my brother-in-law killed Sheila yet?"

"Actually, you might be disappointed yet."

"Oh really? How?"

"I've found out that Randy Folsom had been making some films of some rather risqué society parties and that he was using them for blackmail purposes. That means there's a strong possibility that whoever killed your sister had been trying to get to Folsom, not her."

"That doesn't mean that John didn't do it."

"No, but it enlarges the field of suspects a little."

Her eyes grew curious. "Do you have any specific suspects yet, or is that classified information."

"It's classified information."

"I see." She got up and strolled casually around the room, taking in the sights. That would have normally taken about ten seconds, but she stretched it out to fifteen. She went to the bedroom door, turned on the light, and peeked in. Then she came back over to the couch and sat down and crossed her legs. "Seeing it from the outside, I expected worse."

I didn't know if that were meant to be a compliment or an insult. Probably neither.

"Tell me, Jake, darling, were you surprised to see me when you pulled up?"

"Any Rolls in this neighborhood is good for a shock."

"I wasn't talking about the car and you know it. Were you surprised to see me?"

"I suppose I was, a little. What really surprises me is how you found out where I lived."

She started to say something, but it was drowned out by the sound. It began slowly as a low, distant rumble, then built into a steady, deafening explosion. The windows shook and the cupboards in the kitchen rattled and the glass of bourbon on the coffee table hummed along with the roar. After a few long seconds, it was past.

"What in god's name was that?"

"What time is it?"

She looked at her watch. "Eleven-thirty."

"American Airlines, flight 581, non-stop from Denver."

"You've memorized the schedules?"

"I've lived here for nine months."

"How do you sleep with that going on all night?"

"It doesn't. They've rerouted most of their midnight to seven a.m. flights over the ocean. Besides, it's like the smell. You get used to it."

"I'm afraid I could never get used to it." She handed me her glass. The ice cubes looked very lonely in it. "May I have another, please?"

"It's your scotch."

I went out into the kitchen and made two more drinks. When I came back out, she patted the stained cushion

94

beside her. I sat down obediently and handed her one of the glasses.

"So you found out where I live and that I drink bourbon—"

"I found out a lot more than that. Would you like to hear it?"

I shrugged. I was too tired to fight it.

"I found out you're thirty-four years old, divorced with no children, and a Capricorn. Your father was a tailor who had a little shop down on Fairfax. You graduated from Fairfax High School and then went on to UCLA and quit after two years. You started working for the *Chronicle* in 1960 and were let go in 1969 after being jailed for refusing to reveal your news sources on a story you did. Since that time, you've been working as a private detective. How's that?"

"Not bad. Where'd you manage to dig all of that up?"

She smiled slyly. "I made a few calls to some people I know."

"Why go to all the trouble?"

"If you had answered my questions personally, I wouldn't have had to go to the trouble."

"That still doesn't answer my question."

"Because you fascinate me, Jacob darling, and I'm a woman who knows what she wants. It's as simple as that." She raised her drink to her lips and looked at me over the rim. "One of the calls I made was to Marcus Simon."

"Really? I didn't know you knew him. What did the old fart have to say?"

"Nothing much that was good, I'm afraid. He doesn't seem to share my fondness for you, to say the least. He sounded rather uncomfortable when I asked about you. Wanted to know right away my reasons for asking."

"So what did you tell him?"

"The truth. That you had been around asking about my sister. He warned me about you."

"He's warned a lot of people about me."

"Is it true what he said about you?"

"That depends on what he said."

"That you were brash, loudmouthed, and egotistical and that you were fired because you were insubordinate, quarrelsome, and refused to cooperate with the rest of the staff —quote, unquote."

"I guess the brash and egotistical part is true enough. I might even go along with the loudmouthed part. But the 'fired' garbage was a line of crap he started handing out to cover up his tracks. I was fired because old man Simon started getting scared of the wrath of Big Brother."

"So why didn't you go to another paper after you got out of jail?"

"By that time, the word had already been spread. That same line of bullshit you got had already fallen on the right ears. Marcus Simon's word carries a lot of weight in this town."

"You could always leave town."

"I like L.A. It's my town. And nobody's going to drive me out of it, I don't care what his name is."

I was beginning to feel uncomfortable. I didn't want to talk about me anymore. As a matter of fact, I didn't want to talk at all anymore. My eyelids felt as if they were lined with lead.

"Excuse me a minute, Gloria. I have to call my landlord."

"At this hour?"

"He left a note to call him when I got in. I'm in."

I went into the kitchen and picked up the phone and dialed the number. The voice that answered the ring sounded tired.

"Yes?"

"Mr. Gutierrez, this is Jacob Asch."

The voice perked up. "Yes, Mr. Asch. I'm glad you got my note. Uh, Mr. Asch, I just wanted to let you know that, uh, as of the first of next month, I've leased the house to somebody else. I just wanted to give you your thirty days' notice, as of tonight."

I sat and let it sink in, before answering. "Why? What's happening?"

"Nothing is happening. I was just made an offer I couldn't turn down, you see. Two hundred a month more and a lease. I'm sorry about this, you've always been a good tenant, but you can understand my position."

"Yeah, I understand. So I've got thirty days to move, right?"

"Yes. Thirty days. I'm sorry. I just wanted to let you know right away—"

"Sure, sure. Goodbye, Mr. Gutierrez."

I hung up the phone and came back into the living room and sat down on the couch.

"What's the matter? You look like your best friend just died."

"I'm being goddamn evicted. I've got to be out of here in thirty days."

"But that's illegal. Don't you have a lease?"

"No. That was one of the reasons I took this place. It's month to month."

"Did he give you a reason?"

"Yeah. He said that somebody offered to rent the whole place here for $200 a month more than he was getting now. He said he couldn't turn it down. Jesus Christ, who the hell would want to pay that kind of money for this dump?"

"Where are you going to go?"

"I'll find some place. It's just going to be such a goddamn hassle to move." I was beginning to feel sorry for myself.

She put her drink down and leaned close to me. For a second, the smell of scotch and perfume blended to drown

97

out the smell of jet fuel that lingered in the air. "Poor Jake darling," she murmured, and reached up and pulled my face toward hers. Her lips were warm and soft and her tongue found its way into my mouth and played with my teeth before going in farther to find its mate. With one quick motion, she unzipped the front of her jumpsuit, took my hand, and led it expertly inside. Her breasts were small, but firm. She took a deep breath as I slid my hand across her firm belly and down. The breath turned into a sigh and then a groan as I hooked my finger up and in. We fell back on the couch and I wrestled with the jumpsuit. I had her halfway out of it when she put a hand on my chest and pushed me gently back.

"Let's go into the bedroom."

She picked up her drink with one hand and holding the top of the jumpsuit on with the other, followed me into the bedroom. The last plane of the evening, TWA flight 322 from Kansas City and Albuquerque, flew over at 12:01, but neither of us heard it.

CHAPTER 10

When I woke up the next morning at eight, the smell of jet fuel had once again taken over and the smell of her perfume was gone. In the indentation on the pillow where her head had been, there was a note.

> Jacob darling. Must go. You were wonderful.
> See you soon I hope. Love, Gloria.

I picked up the empty scotch glasses, took them into the kitchen and rinsed them out and put them away. Then I shaved and showered, all the while reliving last night's three-hour debauch.

I made it over to Filmways Equipment Rental by 9:30 and cornered the owner, a Mr. Sam Fields. He told me that he remembered the Folsom case well, that he had sued to recover some camera equipment Folsom had rented and failed to return. The matter had been settled out of court for $2,000. I took down the name of the lawyer who had handled the settlement for Folsom—a Beverly Hills attorney by the name of Phillip Matthies—thanked him and left.

I stopped off at a coffee shop nearby for some scrambled eggs and called Ellman from there to tell him I'd be over to give him the skinny. I was walking out to my car when my eye was caught by a late-model white Ford sedan parked three stalls away. The man sitting behind the steering wheel had a round face, almost like a pie stood on end, and a Pancho Villa mustache. He was wearing glasses fastened to which were those green shade clip-ons that flip up when not in use. There was nothing suspicious about him, nothing at all. He was probably just waiting for his wife to come out of the restaurant. I stored the face in my memory bank and went on.

The receptionist told me that Mr. Ellman was expecting me and to go on in. As I walked through the door, Paul tossed a manila folder on the desk toward me. "There are your driving histories. The list you asked Warren for is there too."

"Good. I've got something for you, too." I took a cassette cartridge out of my coat pocket and handed it to him.

"What's this?"

"I haven't had time to type up a report, so I dictated it. I thought you could have your secretary transcribe it. It's pretty hot stuff, and I'd feel better if it were in a less perishable place than my head."

He got out his tape machine and set it up and while he was listening to my report, I started to go through the driving histories. Folsom had several entries for moving violations, one in 1963 for running a red light, one in 1965 for speeding, one in 1967 for failure to heed a street sign, and four in 1970 for speeding. One of the 1970 tickets had an FTA entry beside it, denoting that he had failed to appear in court and that the ticket had gone to warrant. He had his license pulled for that one. There were no accidents listed.

Sheila Warren had a couple of speeding violations late in the 1960s and there were two accidents listed, one on February 16, 1969, and the other on September 2, 1972. Beside both dates was marked "LA METRO," telling me that suits had been filed and that both had been handled through the downtown court jurisdiction.

I closed up the folder and waited for the tape to finish.

When it was over, Paul looked ecstatic. "Incredible. Fantastic. This could really shake the hell out of a lot of people."

"Yeah. And there's a lot of loose money floating around trying to make sure that none of it ever hits the surface. I've already run into some of it. You know, if you keep on digging into this, you could turn out to be a very unpopular fellow."

"I'm used to not being liked by now. A criminal lawyer gets it from both ends, Jake—you know that. You lose a case and your client threatens to kill you. You defend a murderer and get him off with second degree when you and he both know he should have gotten life, and he calls you up and tells you you should have gotten him acquitted and he's going to come looking for you when he gets out. You get some jerk a not guilty on an armed robbery charge and he calls *you* a goddamn thief and threatens to beat your head in because you charged him some miserable fee that he probably won't ever pay anyway. And the whole time, the public calls you a slick lawyer who's letting killers and rapists go free on legal technicalities and declares you an enemy of the public welfare. If being unpopular worried me, I would have gotten out of this business a long time ago."

"All I'm saying is we had better watch our step, that's all."

"Sure, sure." He sat back and smiled and patted his belly. "Well, things are starting to shape up pretty fast."

"Here's hoping. Oh, I want you to do something for me. See what you can find out about one Phillip Matthies. He's an attorney. Has an office in Beverly Hills."

"What's his story?"

"He was Folsom's lawyer in a civil suit back in 1969. I don't know if there's any connection other than a business one, but I'd like to find out. I thought maybe one of your

101

lawyer buddies might know something about him."

"I'll make some calls."

"Thanks. And get that tape transcribed and put away. By now everybody and his brother knows what we're doing."

CHAPTER 11

By the following Wednesday, I had checked out most of my leads and come up with a big, fat zero. Both Allison Shaw's and Chase Martin's alibis checked out, and although I wasn't ruling them out as suspects, there wasn't much I could work on there. All of the people on Warren's list gave me the same story: No, I haven't the slightest idea who would want to do such a dreadful thing to poor Sheila. . . . She didn't have an enemy in the world. . . . No, I haven't seen Sheila much at all in the past few months. . . . You know, she had become very remote in the past year. . . . Toward the end, I got kind of an eerie feeling being around her. No, I can't describe it, just sort of an odd feeling that she was not really with me, but somewhere far away. . . .

All had expressed a deep sense of shock over Mrs. Warren's untimely and gruesome demise, but I got the distinct impression sitting in those plushly padded living rooms that it was more a mechanical reaction put on for my benefit than any outpouring of genuine emotion. Those posh social gals were probably tickled pink to have some new juicy bit of scandal to snack on over afternoon martinis.

With nowhere to go and nothing to do, I figured I might as well deadend on the driving histories. The court indexes showed that the police report for the September 2, 1972 accident was filed at the downtown station, so I got in my car and drove over.

I handed the police clerk a business card that said I was Albert A. Brooks of the Heartland Life and Casualty Com-

103

pany. I gave her a phony insurance claim number, and she brought me the report.

The accident, it turned out, was a collision on the corner of Figueroa and Olympic. Mrs. Warren had been driving a 1970 Cadillac convertible, estimated speed, 35 miles per hour. She had entered the intersection first, coming down Olympic, when she was hit broadside by a '56 Ford sedan, driven by one John T. Patterson, who had run the red light on Figueroa. There were no injuries, but Patterson was booked on suspicion of drunk driving. According to the report, Patterson was alone at the time of the accident, but Mrs. Warren was not. One Christopher Jonathan Ruane was listed as being Right Front V-1. I jotted down the information I needed and gave the report back to the red-head and left.

I had no idea who this Ruane character was, but Sheila Warren didn't strike me as the type of woman who would have picked up hitchhikers late at night, and the accident had occurred at 1:30 a.m. I decided to go visiting, just to see where it would get me; I had nothing else to do anyway.

Of course, Ruane turned out not to be listed. I was a few blocks away from the Registry of Voters, so I hopped over there to look him up. The records gave three addresses for Christopher J. Ruane: a current one at 116 Miralinda Drive, L.A., and two previous addresses, one in 1968 at 1450 Fair Oak, L.A., and another in 1971, at 39079 Summit View Road, Malibu. He was a Democrat and listed his occupation as "research consultant," whatever that meant. I took down all three addresses and headed over to Miralinda Drive.

The neighborhood was racially mixed, being on the outside or inside edges of black L.A., depending on your frame of reference. Two small black boys who were playing with a rubber ball on the sidewalk, stopped their game of catch and inspected me thoroughly as I walked past the blue Porsche roadster that was parked in the driveway of 116. It was a one-story, white Spanish house with a red tile roof. Black wrought-iron bars covered the front windows and by the door, suspended from the frong porch overhang, was a cheap Mexican pottery planter in which some edgy geraniums were slowly turning brown in the sun. When I rang the bell, the curtains of the front window rustled and parted and I caught a glimpse of a face.

The man who answered the door was Caucasian. He had a long flaccid face which was indelibly marked with the ruts of long-ago acne. His lips were thin and dark, almost purple. He was wearing white loafers with no socks, a pair of low-cut brushed blue denims with a white belt, and a long-sleeved powder-blue shirt open at the throat. A lock of carefully styled brown hair fell across his forehead, and he brushed it away with a flick of his hand.

"Christopher Ruane?"

"Yeah?"

"I'd like to talk to you."

"About what?"

"Sheila Warren."

"I don't know any Sheila Warren."

I was getting tired of that line.

"Don't you read the newspapers? She was killed a few weeks ago."

"I never read the papers. There's nothing but bad news in them. Like this whoever it was you were talking about being murdered. Too depressing."

"I didn't say anything about her being murdered. I said she was killed."

"So I just assumed you meant she was murdered. I still don't know anything about her."

"I think you do."

"So who are you?"

"Just a man doing a job."

His brown eyes squinted up. "Say, what is this? I've

talked to all the goddamn cops I'm going to. You guys got no right to come over here and harass me. I did my thing and now I'm clean. So just lay off."

"Who says I'm a cop?"

He bit his lip. "You look like a cop."

"I'm not a cop. I'm a private investigator and I'd really like to talk to you about Sheila Warren."

"I told you I don't know any Sheila Warren."

"Knew. Past tense. She's dead, remember? You knew her all right. You were a passenger in her car when she got into an accident less than a year ago."

"Find somebody else to make conversation with, buddy. I'm busy."

I had to jump back quickly to keep my nose from being flattened by the slamming door. I stood there for a few seconds, letting it all sink in, then turned to go back to the car. The two small black boys were still there on the sidewalk, watching.

"Hi," I said.

Their silent stares told me I was an intruder here and not welcome. There was no doubt about it; I was a real hit today. I walked on past them and got into the car.

Sheriff's Homicide was on the tenth floor of the old County Hall of Records, one of the few old gray stone buildings in the L.A. Civic Center that had not been torn down and replaced by something that looked like the U.N. The building had a heavy, musty odor, and the only pneumatic elevator left in the city of Los Angeles, which said something about its age. Its days were numbered, however, and most of the tenants, anticipating urban renewal, had moved out and taken their little white letters with them, leaving Sheriff's Homicide and a few others to go down with the ship.

I stepped through the open elevator doors and into the iron cage. A shrunken old man who had seen better days sat in the elevator on a little stool that had also seen better days. His eyes were half-open and glassy, and he seemed to be fighting a battle against sleep. Right now, the battle was a draw. His head would drop, then jerk quickly back up as the chin made its descending arc onto the frail chest. He was wearing his regulation police riot helmet, the same one he had worn to work every day for the past three years, ever since the boys in Sheriff's Homicide had pitched in and given it to him as a Christmas present.

I rapped twice lightly on the top of the helmet. The head came up and the eyes blinked back their drowsiness and came alive.

"Hello, Mr. Asch."

"Hello, Charlie."

"I was just resting my eyes for a minute. Slow morning."

"Sure, Charlie."

He seemed embarrassed at having been caught napping while on guard duty. Charlie took his job very seriously.

"Ten?"

"Yep."

He sprang to life, determined to make up for his former laxity and threw back his shoulders as he yanked the lever. The elevator hissed and took off. He overshot the tenth floor by at least two feet, but too proud to admit defeat, he worked the handle of the great hissing beast until it finally lowered us into position.

"Thanks, Charlie. Good ride."

The old face, redeemed, smiled up at me.

The hallway was empty when I stepped into it. My lonely footsteps echoed off the walls as they flapped against the tiny, white, hexagonal-shaped tile floor. I turned left down a smaller corridor and passed through a doorway marked HOMICIDE DIVISION.

Filing cabinets and WANTED bulletins lined the perimeter of the large room, the center of it being filled with tables,

107

each about ten feet long, generously littered with arrest reports, memos and miscellaneous sheets of paper. Facing each other across each table were three pairs of plain-clothes partners, each pair sharing a phone which sat between them. On the left was a row of cheap wooden partitions—termed "offices" by the staff.

Lieutenant Albert Herrera was sitting at his desk in his ten foot by ten foot cubicle, going through some morgue shots.

His broad face beamed when I came in, and he stood up and held out a meaty hand. His tie was loose and his massive neck rose out of the collar of his pale blue short-sleeved shirt like a brown tree trunk. Herrera was one of the valuable contacts I'd made from the *Chronicle*, and one of the few I'd managed to keep. He was all cop—one who did his job straight down the line and didn't take any shit from anybody, which is probably the best kind of cop there is.

"How you been, kid?" he asked. "Pull up a chair and tell me what's on your mind."

I ripped a sheet of paper off my notepad, printed Ruane's name on it and handed it to him. "I'd like a small favor, Al. Have that guy checked out for me, will you? Run him through C.I.I. and see if there's anything in the local files. I want F.I. cards, vice stuff, anything you've got on him. I think he might have been in a scrape lately."

"What makes you think so?"

"I just paid him a little visit. He was pretty paranoid. Thought I was a cop and started babbling something about the police having no right to harass him. It sounded like he was just up on some kind of rap."

"Easy enough to find out. When do you need the information?"

"As soon as I can get it."

"What are you trying to get a case on this guy for?"

"I'm working for Paul Ellman. He's defending John Warren."

Herrera lifted an intrigued eyebrow. "I thought it was open and shut."

"It may or may not be."

"Where does this guy fit in?"

"I don't know yet. I just didn't like his reactions when I asked him about Sheila Warren. I'm sure that he knew her, but he wouldn't admit it. He seemed nervous when I asked him about her. He refused to answer questions after finding out that I wasn't a cop, and slammed the door in my face."

"He might have known her and just didn't want to get involved."

"Maybe. That's what I want to find out."

"Anything else I can do for you?"

I hesitated, rubbing a finger back and forth across my chin. "As a matter of fact there is. See if you can find out if any eight-millimeter films were entered on any evidence sheets up at the Warren house. Either booked as evidence or filed as inventory."

"Hmmm," he murmured thoughtfully. "That might be a little more difficult. The D.A.'s got all that information. It'd be in the Intelligence files, but all those are top security. Working slob cops like me don't have access. But I'll ask around. Maybe somebody knows something."

"Great," I said. "How are Rose and the kids?"

He seemed glad I asked. "Fine. My oldest just graduated junior high a few weeks ago. We're getting goddamn old, Jake."

"You're telling me."

"Hey, you hear what happened to Peterson last week? Funny as hell. He was transferred over to Hollenbeck a few months ago, ya know. Anyway, they'd been getting a lot of muggings over in Lincoln Heights for the past couple of months. Little old ladies getting knocked over the head and their purses snatched, always in the same two block radius. Well, Peterson and his partner were assigned the case. So they get dressed up like old ladies—dresses, wigs, nylons with the hairs sticking through, the whole bit—and they start walking up and down the street at night to see if they can get mugged. Peterson's walking up one side of the street and his partner's walking down the other side. So pretty soon, here comes this car cruising down the street real slow, ya know, and it pulls over to the curb beside Peterson and the guy leans out the window and propositions Peterson. Peterson sticks his head inside the car window and knows right away this isn't the asshole they're looking for, cause they've got a good description and this guy doesn't match. So he tells the guy to get lost in no uncertain terms. Well, this guy gets mad. He lays rubber up the street and then Peterson sees him hang a U at the top of the block and spin around and the car jumps the curb on the other side of the street and starts heading fifty miles an hour, mowing down parking meters, heading at his partner. Peterson sees this guy trying to run down his partner, so he whips his six-incher out of his purse and as the asshole goes by, puts six slugs into the car. In the meantime, his partner has jumped into a doorway and pulled out his six-incher and has started blasting away. Peterson said you should have seen the look on this guy's face. His mouth was open and his eyes were wide open and he really looked like he didn't even believe it. Two defenseless old ladies opening up on him with .357's. You can't trust anybody anymore. Anyway, they catch this dude in Hollywood ten minutes later; he'd been so scared they estimated he must have been driving a hundred miles an hour to get there in that short of a time. It turns out he really wasn't the mugger. He was some poor guy who'd been out all night drinking, looking for a broad. He'd gotten shut down by every chick

110

he'd met and when the little old lady shut him down, too, he went bananas. His self-image crumbled. When he saw the other little old lady on the other side of the street, he tried to run her down out of spite."

I laughed. "You guys sure get 'em."

"Tell me about it." The smile faded. "Hey, you going to fill me in if you dig up anything on this Warren thing?"

"You'll be the first to know—believe me. Who else would I give the bust to?"

"I'll give you a call at your house tonight. I should have this stuff by then."

"Thanks. Take it easy, hotshot. And don't try to pick up on any strange men on your way home tonight. You can't move that ass around as fast as Peterson. You might get run over."

CHAPTER 12

When I got to the front door, I could hear the phone ringing inside. I leaned the bag of groceries against the wall and fumbled with my keys in the darkness of the driveway. I got the right one on the second try and in three bounds I had the phone. It was Al.

"Jake? You were right about this Ruane dude. He was busted on November tenth, last year. Violation of Section 11530.5 of the State Penal Code."

"Speak English."

"Possession of marijuana for resale. The narcs were staking out a house they had the word was a dropoff point, and they saw this guy Ruane leave it with a large package. They tailed him back to 116 South Miralinda Drive and busted him there. They didn't have a search warrant, but get this —the jerk invites them in and says: 'Make it quick, I got someplace to go.' They found the package under the kitchen sink—a kilo of grass—and another kilo stashed in the living room. They also found some coke and a 9-mm Browning automatic, unregistered."

"What happened to him?"

"He got off easy. Pled guilty and got a year's probation and a $500 fine. The illegal possession of firearms and the cocaine charges were dropped."

"Interesting."

"Yeah. And that isn't all. Your friend also likes fag joints. L.A. Vice has a couple of F.I. cards filed on him, one last year and one the year before. They were both written in the

112

same place, a bar down on Melrose called the Trojan Horse. It's a dive that specializes in rough trade. Good for a couple of knifings a month. They come down on the hole usually twice a year or so, but it just opens back up again when things loosen up. Ruane was there when the vice boys raided the joint. Oh, about the film at the Warren place—"

My ears perked up. "Yeah?"

"I've asked around, but nobody seems to know anything."

"Thanks for trying."

"If you happen to find out anything, you'd better let me in on it."

"I told you you'd be the first to know."

"I'd better be."

"You will. Thanks again for the info."

I hung up and went outside to retrieve my groceries. I washed the spinach and romaine, tossed myself a large salad, and sat down at the breakfast table with a block of sharp cheddar cheese and a cold beer.

After I finished it all off, I felt better. I dumped the dishes in the sink and ran some water over them, popped the tab on another beer, and went into the bedroom to get undressed. I was down to my underwear and socks when the phone rang. I picked up the extension and said hello.

The line was silent. I said hello two, three times more, but nobody answered. I was about to give it up as a wrong number, when I thought I heard something, a faint rustle.

Then I heard the voices. They were faint at first, but then they got louder, as if somebody had turned up the volume. They weren't talking to me, but to each other. I thought maybe the phone company had fouled up and accidentally spliced me into a party-line call, but then I heard a familiar name and I felt the hair on my arms start to rise.

". . . . what are you going to do with us? . . . please, don't . . . Randy, what are they going to do to us? . . ."

There was an interruption in the voices, as if they had been blotted out by something or someone, and then a man's voice: "For chrissakes, what are you going to do (interruption)? What are those things for? You're not going to put that thing on me . . . shut up, Sheila! Just do what they say. . . ."

More interruptions.

The woman screamed. The scream was loud and agonizing. I nearly dropped the phone. The screaming kept up for a good twenty seconds and I thought my nerves were going to snap, but then it subsided into a loud sobbing.

The man's voice: "For chrissakes, she doesn't know! She's telling you the goddamn truth! I'll tell you, I'll tell you. Just let us go. Look, we're not going to tell anybody. Really."

I wanted to hang up, but I couldn't. I was mesmerized by the horror show on the other end of the line.

There were some scuffling noises, some more sobs, some indecipherable rantings by the woman, and then an indescribable sound that made me shiver. It sounded as if it were coming from the man, but I couldn't really tell. It was like no sound I'd ever heard before. It was deep and throaty, as if he were trying to scream but couldn't, as if something had been forced down his throat and he was gagging and trying to scream at the same time. Then there was a shot.

The screaming and sobbing of the woman was louder now, then faded. She said something that was incoherent. (More interruptions.) Then her sobbing gave way to pleading which built in intensity until it was at an hysterical pitch.

". . . please . . . no, please . . . please, please, no, please, no, no, I'll never tell, PLEASE!"

The scream that reached me was more of a high-pitched wail than a scream, the hopeless shriek of somebody desperately giving up life. There was another shot. Then silence.

The silence on the other end of the line was deafening, echoed by the silence of my own living room, and all I could hear was the sound of my own blood thumping in my ears. All my senses were incredibly acute. Sight, smell, touch, taste, a thousand sensory impressions bombarded my body. Then, far away, I heard it. It was a laugh, muffled and distant.

There was a click and the dial tone drowned out the sound of my own blood. My hand was still frozen on the receiver, the knuckles squeezed white, and it was a few seconds before I managed to let it slowly down on its cradle.

I sat down hard on the edge of the bed and tried to pull my mind together. For the last minute or so, I had been listening to Randy Folsom and Sheila Warren die. Whoever had done the job had been thoughtful enough to bring a tape recorder up to the house and tape the whole thing. That ruled out a crime of passion. That tape was the chilling product of a sharp, calculating, very, very sick mind.

I tried to wring out my mind, to remember exactly what I'd heard while it was still fresh, but all my ears kept giving me was an instant replay of that insane laugh. I went out to the kitchen, poured myself a double slug of bourbon, then another, and went back into the bedroom. I opened the top drawer of the bureau, took out the Colt .45 automatic Commander model and a clip. I loaded the clip, inserted it into the butt of the gun, cocked a bullet into the chamber, then let the hammer down slowly with my thumb. Then I put the gun down on the end table by the bed and picked up the phone and dialed Ellman's home number. He got it on the third ring.

"Hello?"

"Paul, this is Jake."

"Yeah, Jake. What's up?"

"Sorry to disturb you this late, but I just thought you'd like to know you're right."

"Right? About what?"

"John Warren not killing his wife. I just got a call from who did it."

There was a stunned pause. "Wha—Wait a minute, wait a minute. What are you talking about?"

"Whoever killed Folsom and Warren just called me up on the phone, goddamn it, and played me a tape recording of Sheila Warren and Randy Folsom dying. Whoever did this thing is a real freak, Paul, and I mean freak!"

"Calm down now, Jake, and try to think. What did the whole thing sound like?"

"Folsom and Warren were talking to their killers. Some screams. A couple of shots. The splicing was uneven and there were blank spots on the tape, as if there had been other voices on the tape, but they'd been erased. Folsom and Sheila Warren were erased in parts, too."

"You think the erasures might have been parts where they called the killers by name?"

"That was my thought, too. And if that's right, they all knew one another. One thing for sure, there was more than one of them. At one point, Folsom said: 'Do what *they* say.'"

"Let's call the cops. This will prove to those bastards—"

"It isn't going to prove anything to anybody. They won't believe us. They'll say it's some kind of stunt we've cooked up to get some favorable publicity for Warren."

"What do you think we should do?"

"The same thing we've been doing. That call was meant to scare me off, which means we're getting close to something somebody doesn't want us close to. If we don't get scared off, maybe they'll try again. I'm going to put a tap

116

on one of my own phones here, just in case. Then we will have something tangible to take to the cops."

"You think they might try to take a crack at you?"

"I don't know. I don't think so. If they wanted to do that, they could have done it a lot easier without warning me off first. I've got my gun out of mothballs anyway."

"You got a permit to carry it?"

"Hell, no. Why, do you know a friendly chief of police who would issue me one?"

"You're on better terms with the cops than I am."

"None of the cops I'm friendly with have the authority to issue concealed weapons permits. Even if they could, I don't think they would."

"Well, just be careful."

"Anybody who tries to get in here is going to get his head blown off."

After another stiff drink, I felt kind of lightheaded and went to bed. I couldn't have been asleep an hour when I woke up bathed in a cold sweat. Somebody was chuckling faintly in the corner. My hand slid over the bed table and found the handle of the .45 and I pointed it, shaking, into the darkness and snapped on the light. Nothing. It took me a while to get back to sleep. I'm not used to sleeping with the lights on.

CHAPTER 13

I woke up exhausted. I struggled up, turned out the lights, and staggered into the bathroom to try to get my act together. I splashed some cold water in my face and went into the kitchen to get some coffee. I located the instant, put on the kettle to boil, decided that would take too long, and took the hot water from the tap. After two more cups and a hot-cold needle shower, I felt half-human. After an English muffin, I felt three-quarters human. Once my brain started functioning again, I mapped out my agenda for the day. Christopher Ruane was on the top of the list.

As I turned on Miralinda, I saw the Porsche back out of Ruane's driveway and head down the street. Just for fun, I followed. He turned on Third Street and pulled into the parking lot of the Little Kettle Coffee Shop. I swung around and parked on the far side of the building and went in through the back door.

The cashier was a smiling, friendly girl, and I asked her for change. She gave it to me and I went outside and bought a paper and came back in. I kept an eye on Ruane from the protection of the cash register. He was sitting with another man in a booth by the window. The other man was dressed in a black suit and white shirt, a sharp contrast to Ruane's flowery open-necked shirt and bell-bottoms, and he was older, maybe forty. He had dark, bushy eyebrows that joined together over the nose. The nose itself was large, and the nostrils flared. It gave the impression of being an awning for his mouth. I bet myself he could have smoked a cigar in the shower.

The man with the nose wasn't saying much, but was just sitting there listening and nodding. Then Ruane pushed a folded newspaper across the table to him and the man picked it up and stuck it under his arm and rose. Ruane threw some change on the table and slid out of the booth.

I turned quickly and went back to the car. Ruane I figured I could always find, so I decided that I had better follow the stranger. The meeting had aroused my curiosity. I realized, of course, that it could all just be my suspicious nature acting up again, that the entire episode could be nothing more than two ex-college chums meeting to engage in a nice, one-sided, five-minute chat over coffee. Or maybe the mysterious stranger was a bookie to whom Ruane was slipping the sports section of the paper on which were secretly marked his selections for tomorrow's races. But then the man did not look like a bookie somehow. Or an ex-college chum.

I came out of the driveway and waited by the corner. The Porsche drove out first, heading back down Santa Monica in the direction it had come. A beige '63 Chevy pulled out directly behind the Porsche and as it passed I recognized the nose. I took down the license number and started off, keeping a block or so behind in order to avoid being spotted. But I played it wrong and stayed too far behind. I saw the light turn yellow and saw the Chevy speed up and sail through it and I knew I wasn't going to make it. I sat hitting the steering wheel with the palms of my hands, calling the red light all sorts of dirty names while trying to keep the beige car in sight. It was no use. The gods must have been against me. By the time I jumped the green light, I was stopped cold by another red one at the next corner, and the Chevrolet was long gone. I turned around and headed back toward Ruane's house, thinking that from the direction he had gone, he might have returned home.

I was right, the blue Porsche sat quietly in the same spot in the driveway, as if it had never left.

The street was deserted and silent, the two boys with the ball nowhere in sight. I rang again. Then once more. The curtains rustled and were still. Ruane took a while opening the front door and when he finally did, he stood there projecting pure hatred. It was enough to make me feel unloved.

"Remember me?"

"I remember you."

"I'd still like to talk."

"I thought I got my point across that the feeling wasn't mutual."

"You did. But my ego just wouldn't let me believe it. How could anybody possibly not want to talk to me?"

He tried to shut the door, but I wasn't about to let the same thing happen twice. I stuck my foot in it and shouldered my way past him into the living room.

"Nice little place you've got here," I said, looking around.

The room was not large, but looked smaller than it really was due to the amount of furniture in it. A couch sat in the center of everything, covered by some sort of thick fur throw-rug. There was a coffee table in front of this on which sat assorted lighters, ashtrays and a green Chinese incense burner with a roaring lion on top of it. There were three Spanish leather chairs and a dining room set, complete with mahogany table and chairs and a glass-front cabinet in which sat some delicate and expensive-looking china.

I flopped down on the couch and ran my hand over the fur. It was soft. Ruane looked like the kind that would like soft things. Ruane had followed me in and stood in front of me looking rather perturbed. As he stood there, I noticed for the first time, the sickeningly thick, sweet smell of perfume.

"What the hell is this? Get the fuck out of here before I call the police."

"Go ahead," I said, smiling. "Call them. I bet they like me better than they like you."

He went over to the phone and picked up the receiver.

"Oh, and while you've got them on the phone, let me talk to them. I've got something they might be interested in."

He stopped dialing and looked up.

"Yesterday you told me you were clean."

"I am clean."

"Really?"

He hadn't resumed dialing.

"Look, Ruane, all I want are some answers to a few very simple questions. Answer the questions, and I'll leave you alone. Otherwise, you might find yourself back in hot water."

"You don't scare me."

"I'm not trying to. I'm just trying to tell you where it's at."

He hesitated, then put the phone slowly back down. "What if you don't like my answers?"

"We'll cross that bridge when we come to it."

"How do I know you'll leave me alone afterwards?"

"You don't. All you know for sure is that if you don't answer the questions, I won't leave you alone."

He looked at his watch and then back up at me. "Okay, but let's make this quick. I've got somewhere to go."

That was the identical line that got him put in the slammer the last time. I just hoped lightning would strike twice in the same place.

He sat down in a chair facing me, crossed his legs, and

lit a cigarette from the box on the table. All of his movements were smooth and fluid, consummated with a catlike grace.

"How did you happen to know Sheila Warren?"

"I met her early last year in Beverly Hills at the Key Club."

"So why did you try to tell me you'd never heard of her?"

"I just didn't want to get involved in a murder case. Why should I? I've been in trouble once before and I know there would be no sense in getting mixed up in something that heavy."

"So you knew her from the Key Club?"

"I wouldn't say knew. I met her there. She was alone one night and I was alone. She came up and asked me to dance. She told me she was married, and that her husband didn't understand her—all that standard crap. She was drunk and hot to trot. We left together. She suggested we take a drive in her car and then go to her place. I thought it would be a quickie, you know? Then she plowed into another car and sobered up pretty quick, took me back to my car, and that was that. I never saw her again."

"How about Randy Folsom? You ever meet him?"

"Who's he?"

"The man who was murdered with Mrs. Warren."

"Never heard of him."

"What kind of job do you have, Ruane, that you're home in the afternoon all the time? You work nights?"

"No. I'm a technical consultant for International Synthetics. I go to the plant only a couple of days a week. Most of my work I do at home."

"You've got a nice little place here. You must get a pretty good salary."

"What are you getting at?"

"Mrs. Warren was known to have been dabbling with drugs."

"So?"

"You never sold her any?"

"I was never dealing. Not that kind of dealing."

"What was the kilo they found at your house?"

"I used to help out a few friends, that's all. I never sold anything to anybody I didn't consider a close friend."

"So that one time at the Key Club was the one and only time you saw Sheila Warren."

"That's right."

"And you just thought she would be a hot piece of ass—that's why you went along with her?"

"That's right," he said, blowing a series of tiny smoke rings from his O-shaped mouth.

"Well, there's just one thing that doesn't fit in. What would a fag want with a hot piece of ass?"

He put the cigarette down, and jerked himself out of his chair, "Get out of here, motherfucker, before I break your head open."

"Please," I said as I stood up, "I abhor violence. But I haven't met a fag yet that could break my head open."

His features grew suddenly calm. He walked over to the fireplace and picked up a poker, testing the weight of it in his hand. "You never met a fag with a poker, then, punk. Now move on out of here before I get mad."

"But you're so beautiful when you're angry," I said, backing slowly out of the living room until I reached the front door. The door slammed shut but my nose was well out of range this time.

I had handled that one badly. I had made myself conspicuous in exchange for very little information. All I had found out was that Ruane had lied, that he had known Mrs. Warren better than he cared to admit, something I'd known all along. The exchange had been a bad one and in this business bad exchanges like that could turn out to be very dangerous.

As I drove up the block, my thoughts were turned from Ruane to a late-model white Ford sedan that was parked by the curb. As I passed, the driver turned his head, but not quickly enough to keep me from getting a look at his face.

CHAPTER 14

I hadn't checked with my answering service for three days, so before I left the house the next morning, I called. They had one message: a Brian Whittaker had called four times yesterday and said that it was very important he get in touch with me. He left a number.

Brian Whittaker turned out to be the Whittaker part of Cohen, Whittaker, and Bernstein, attorneys at law. He told me he had a matter he would like to talk over with me, but that he'd rather not discuss it over the phone. Could I come to his office. I said no, but I'd be in my office in an hour and gave him directions how to get there.

Everything in the office was exactly the same as I'd left it a week ago. The hotplate was still sitting on the edge of the scarred, gray top of the desk and the Silex was still on it, half-full of water. Some typed reports were scattered over the rest of the desk, covered with the circular brown stains of sloppy coffee drinking. The two hardwood chairs were unmoved, the filing cabinet was still in the corner of the room, and my only valuable possession—a fifth of Wild Turkey—was still in the double safe. The only thing that had really changed was the window behind my desk that looked down on Seventh Street—it was a little grimier. But that was okay; there wasn't anything on Seventh Street to look at anyway except for more of the same old dirty-brown buildings like the one I was in.

I turned on the hotplate and went down the hall to the bathroom. By the time I got back, the water was hot and I got my mug and the jar of instant coffee out of the desk drawer and settled down to wait for Brian Whittaker.

He came in about twenty minutes later. He was dark-complected and short and had a narrow, shrewlike face. He was carrying a black leather attaché case and was wearing a three-piece, gray wool suit that looked like it could have been custom-made.

"Mr. Asch?"

"Mr. Whittaker?"

He had been smiling when he hit the door, but the smile seemed to grow a little forced as he was hit by the full impact of the office.

"Sit down, Mr. Whittaker. Coffee?"

"No, thank you," he said. "I'll try not to waste any more of your time than I have to and get right to the point." He sat down and swung the attaché case onto his lap, hit the buttons and the locks sputtered open. He reached in and took out a rectangular slip of yellow paper and held it up in the murky light that filtered painfully through the window at my back. "This is a cashier's check for five thousand dollars, Mr. Asch. It's yours in exchange for a small service."

"Who do you want me to kill?"

"Nothing that drastic, I can assure you."

"Sorry, Mr. Whittaker, but at the present time I'm all tied up with a case."

He put the check down on the desk and stared at it. We both stared at it. For different reasons, I assumed.

"I know. It is because of your involvement with the Warren case, in fact, that I'm offering you the money. Both jobs are related, although tangentially, to one another."

"Who's offering me this money?"

"My client wishes to remain anonymous for various reasons."

"Exactly what do you want done?"

126

"My client is interested in recovering certain films that were up at the Warren estate. Movies of the eight-millimeter variety."

"You want me to recover some of Randy Folsom's artwork."

"That is correct."

"There are other operatives in this city who are free at the present time who would be more than happy to take the job, Mr. Whittaker. You might have better luck with them. I could give you a couple of names—"

"We already have other detectives working on this. You're not the only one we've contacted. But we thought that since you were working close to the whole matter, you might stumble on to something. My client wishes to be covered in case of such an eventuality."

"And this client's name is?"

"I told you he wishes to remain anonymous."

"Anybody who sends his messenger boys to bribe me forgoes that privilege."

The shrew features grew sterner, sharper. "I am *not* a messenger boy, Mr. Asch, and this is *not* a bribe. My client wishes to *employ* you to recover—"

"Let's call a spade a spade. Whoever it is that sent you over here wants to bribe me to protect his or her lily-white reputation so that he can hold his head up at the country club without worrying that somebody's going to blow the lid off and expose him for what he really is."

He pointed to the check, his voice steady and confident. "That's five thousand dollars there."

"Hooray."

"Look, Asch—"

"Save it. You can tell your client I haven't found the films."

"Well, if you do happen to find them, we are prepared to give you the five thousand."

He was like a suit of wet sand, and he was starting to rub me raw. "The answer is still no. Listen, those films might just be crucial to my client's case and if I found them and turned them over to you, there might just be something involved called conflict of interests. I like money, but not that much. There happens to be a man sitting in the County Jail with his life on the line. You can call it sentimentality, humanitarianism, altruism, or any fucking thing you want, but that happens to be more important to me than some society freak who's flipped out on kinky sex and who wants to be sheltered from the wrath of the horrible, wicked public. So you can go back to Mystery Challenger Number Three and tell him he can stick his check up his nose and light it."

It was a great speech, moving and dramatic, but it had about as much impact on him as a BB gun on the Queen Mary. "If you do recover the films, and they turn out *not* to be important to your case, you can then turn them over to me for the stipulated amount."

"It's unbelievable. I think you really must be deaf. Why don't you just get out of my office and let me have a little peace?"

He shrugged, put the check back in his attaché case and stood up. "You know your trouble? You think cheap. I suppose you'll enjoy spending the rest of your life in this dismal little office, running down petty insurance claims for a few hundred dollars a throw."

"Better than I'd like what's attached to that check."

"Everybody has his price."

"That's probably true. What's the price of a new bridge, Whittaker? If I knock all your teeth out, do you think Mr. Cohen or Mr. Bernstein would handle my case, or do you think they might consider it a conflict of interest?"

He muttered something unintelligible and scurried through the door.

I sat with my hand wrapped around the coffee mug, glowing with self-righteousness, listening to his footsteps die in the hallway. By the time they were no longer audible, the self-righteousness had given way to annoyance. That bright yellow slip of paper was suspended in the air where Whittaker had held it up, glowing.

I looked around at the oatmeal-gray walls and swore. He was right. That damn jerk was right. This office *was* dismal. I wondered what it was inside me that killed any chance that came up to leave this hole. The answer came glibly, without hesitation: Once you start sliding down that long, muddy hill, Asch, there's nothing but a dirty puddle at the bottom. But what was I in if it wasn't a dirty puddle? I toyed with the idea, only half-seriously, of calling Whittaker's office and leaving a message to call, but let that one go. I went over to the safe and dialed the combination, took out the Wild Turkey, and poured a shot in my coffee. By the time I was down to the bottom of the cup, the check had stopped glowing. I repeated the sequence and three-quarters of the way through the second cup, the check was gone. I put the Wild Turkey back in the safe, picked my coat from the back of my chair and went down to the street.

I got my car and drove over to the Department of Motor Vehicles to check out Ruane's coffee companion. The girl ran the Chevy's license number through the computer and came up with a Ronald S. Eberhardt of 662 South Benton Way, Hollywood. I gave her my seventy-five cents and left.

Benton Way ran off Vine for about two blocks, solid with cheap apartment buildings. Six hundred sixty-two was a chunky, two-story job, one of the kind with silver flecks mixed in with the plaster so that when the sunlight hit it at the right angle, it glittered like a two-dollar whore with delusions of grandeur.

Eberhardt's name was on the Apartment 6 mailbox. I went up the outside stairs and knocked, but nobody answered, so I came back down and knocked on the manager's door. I told the manager, a Mrs. Rosenberg, that my name was Ernest Goldstein from the Department of Urban Planning and that I was collecting statistical information on the neighborhood and wondered if she could answer a few questions for me. As soon as she heard the name Goldstein, she invited me in.

She turned out to be a compulsive talker. By the time I left an hour later, I'd found out that Eberhardt was a nice, quiet man who usually kept to himself and always paid his rent on time. He was a driver for Brown Brothers Mortuary on Wilshire, and apart from that, the only peculiar thing about him was that he kept odd hours—sometimes three, four, even five in the morning. Mrs. Rosenberg knew that because he lived directly above her and often woke her up coming in. I also had backgrounds on the building's nineteen other tenants, a full account of Mrs. Rosenberg's move West, and a detailed description of her husband's death in a tragic drowning accident.

Brown Brothers Funeral Chapel occupied space on a not-too-fashionable section of Wilshire Boulevard and was not the kind of mortuary you see advertised all over the city on bus benches. It was an old, two-story building onto which somebody had slapped a colonial-style, red brick false front, complete with fake portico over the double white front doors. I rang the bell.

The door was opened by a jockey-sized man dressed in work khakis. A vacuum cleaner whined loudly behind him.

"I'd like to see whoever's in charge."

"What?"

"I'd like to see whoever's in charge."

"Just a minute." He disappeared for a few seconds and the whine of the vacuum cleaner died. "Now, what is it you want?"

"I'd like to see whoever's in charge." I handed him a card.

"That's Mr. Peeples. Come in."

The greeting hall was spacious and smelled of the dust resurrected by the vacuum cleaner. The walls were pale blue and the carpeting, which was wearing thin in spots, was almost navy. In the center of the room, three sofas were clustered around a coffee table on which sat a vase of plastic flowers. Over the fireplace was a painting of an old Italian mariner who was looking intently at a sextant. All in all, it looked like there was longevity in the neighborhood.

The jockey told me to sit down and ambled off down the hall. He returned a few seconds later, trailed by another man. This one was short, but not as short as the jockey, and stocky. He had full cheeks and plenty of wiry brown hair that had a hint of red in it. He wore glasses, a wide-lapeled brown suit that looked like it had come into style only after it had gone out once, and a faintly soured expression. I assumed the soured expression was permanent and not worn for my benefit.

"I'm Mr. Peeples," he said, offering his hand. "What can I do for you?"

Before I could answer, the jockey had started up the vacuum cleaner and was pushing it over the carpet. Mr. Peeples threw him an annoyed glance and suggested we adjourn to his office.

The office was down the hall and to the right. It was narrow and windowless and was painted lime green. On top of the desk a copy of some mortician's trade magazine was open to an ad for a "Monte Carlo, a Duraseal metal casket by the Rayburn Company of Detroit," which had a "Fog-Mist Finish, interior lavishly lined in 600 Red Cheney Velvet, lushly quilted and shirred, with matching King-Size bolster and coverlet." Mr. Peeples put the magazine in one

131

of the desk drawers and sat down. "Now, what can I help you with, Mr. Asch?"

"I believe you have a driver working for you by the name of Ronald Eberhardt."

"Yes."

"How long has he been working for you?"

"Seven years, I think. Yes, seven years this September."

"And he's a hearse driver, is that correct?"

"We don't call them hearses here, Mr. Asch. We refer to them as coaches. But yes, you're correct, he is my driver."

"What kind of an employee is he?"

"Fine. Reliable. Otherwise he wouldn't have worked for me for seven years, would he? Why? What's this all about?"

"I'm just running a little credit check on him, that's all. He's buying a television and he's applied for credit. It's standard procedure."

"Oh."

"I'd like to talk to him, if I could."

"Didn't your company already talk to him when he applied for credit?"

"Yes, but there are a few minor things I have to check on."

He looked suspicious. "Don't you think it would be better for your company's public relations if you visited people at their homes, instead of bothering them during working hours?"

"It won't take long, Mr. Peeples. I just want to ask him a couple of questions."

"I have a firm policy that I never allow my employees to have visitors during working hours. It just so happens that he happens to be out on a call now, anyway."

"Oh. Well, I'll try to get him at his place later on. Can you tell me his working hours?"

"Nine to five. Unless we get a call, of course."

"I'll try to catch him after work. Sorry to have disturbed you, Mr. Peeples."

I left the office, went through the greeting hall and out the front door. I started down the block to my car, but I was stopped by a small stream of soapy water that was running down the mortuary driveway into the street. I followed the water up the driveway to its source, a cemented courtyard out back. On one side of the courtyard, facing the back of the building, was a shelter partitioned off into three separate stalls. Powder-blue Cadillac hearses were parked in two of the stalls, and a darker blue Ford van was in the third. Someone was in one of the stalls, a soapy sponge in one hand and a hose in the other, washing down one of the Cadillacs.

"Hello," I said.

He looked up from his work. It was Eberhardt.

"My name's Jacob Asch. I'm a private investigator." I showed him my I.D.

"Yeah?"

"I'd like to talk to you, if you could spare a minute."

"What about?"

"Christopher Ruane."

"Who?"

"Christopher Ruane."

"Don't know anybody by that name," he said, and ran some water over the last bit of suds left on the hood of the hearse.

"Okay. Maybe he used another name. What was the name of the guy you were having coffee with at the Little Kettle Coffee Shop on Third Street a couple of mornings ago? The guy that gave you the newspaper?"

His eyes grew very still. He licked his lips. "What newspaper? I never been in anyplace called the Little Kettle. You must have me mistaken for somebody else."

"No. Nobody else."

His hand was trembling slightly. He turned his back on me and turned off the hose, then started winding it into a coil on the ground by the water faucet. "Look, I'm telling you you have the wrong guy, okay? So beat it."

I was going to keep on him, but I was stopped by a voice behind me. "I thought I told you I didn't want my employees being bothered during working hours."

I turned around. Mr. Peeples was glaring at me through his glasses.

"You also told me he was out on a call."

"He was. He must have gotten back a little while ago without me knowing. Are you calling me a liar?"

"I wouldn't do a thing like that."

"I'm going to have to ask you to vacate these premises immediately, Mr. Asch, otherwise I shall call the police. You're trespassing."

"Okay. Have it your way."

I left them both there with the coiled hose and the coaches, and went down the driveway to the street.

CHAPTER 15

I still wasn't ready to give up on Ruane. I went over to Andre's and took my time over dinner, then headed over to the Trojan Horse. I parked on Melrose, a block below the club, and walked back.

The front of the Trojan Horse was painted purple and was sandwiched between two groupings of dirty storefront. A neon sign blinked onoff, onoff above the entranceway: ALL MALE DANCE REVUE.

A couple of leather-jacketed sidewalk commandos trying to look like bikers were hanging around the outside, smoking, and they looked me over approvingly as I went in.

It was dark inside and the room was full of people and sweat and cigarette smoke. A rainbow-colored jukebox blasted out a Jerry Lee Lewis song from the corner, and next to it a short-haired, well-muscled young man, clad only in black tights, his chest glistening with chicken fat, was dancing on stage. In the center of the room, some butches dressed in windbreakers and jeans were dancing with more femme-looking girls and at the tables along the walls, other lesbian couples were kissing and playing grabbie under the table.

I walked over to the bar. The bartender looked as if he would have felt more at home behind the wheel of a Semi than polishing glasses. But that was always the way.

"Bourbon and water."

"Beer or wine."

"Beer."

"Ole, Coors, or Michelob on tap."

"Coors."

He came back with a glass and a bottle of Coors. "Dollar."

"For a lousy beer?"

He pointed to the go-go dancer on stage. "You got to pay something for entertainment."

"I forgot about the entertainment," I said and dished out a buck.

A kid who looked a lot like the dancer on the stage except for the tin splint that was holding his nose together, sidled up to the bar and ordered a beer. The bartender gave him one. "Dollar-ten."

The kid pulled out a bill and some change and put it down on the bar. I wondered why he'd been charged ten cents more for a beer than I had and then I looked down and saw. The set of keys that hung from the belt of his pants were on the left side. That and the splint on his nose told me he was the M side of S-M.

"Hi."

"Bye."

"You're not very friendly."

"I know. And you don't have any noses left to play around with."

He turned his splint in the air and shoved off to the far side of the room where a dozen replicas of the punks outside were shooting pool and making a hell of a racket doing it.

I moved with my beer through the maze of tables toward the pool tables. I was working my way around the edge of the dance floor when I saw Ruane. He was sitting at a table with two leather boys, drinking a glass of red wine. One of the pair, a heavy-set bearded slob with long, stringy hair, was leaning over toward him and talking and Ruane was laughing, but his laughter abruptly halted when he saw me. He said something to the other two, pointed to me, and went out past the pool games and through a door that said: EXIT—REST ROOMS. I set my beer down on a table and hurried after him, but Ruane's bearded friend stood up and bumped into me.

"Hey, man, like I'm really sorry."

I tried to move around him, but he blocked my way, and when I moved to the left, he moved to the left. I grabbed him by both shoulders and slammed him back down in his chair and ran out the back door. It opened into a small, grimy alleyway that ran out to Melrose. I started to run, but I stopped when I saw two of the sidewalk commandos appear in the mouth of the alley. I turned around. Four more, including the bearded one at the table, were out the back door and coming up toward me. I didn't think I was going to like this at all. A lump of fear started to congeal in my throat and my heart started beating fast. I looked around, saw nothing but dirty alley walls, and felt myself being slowly overtaken by a creeping terror that was starting to work its way down my body, into my arms and legs, threatening to paralyze me.

"Where you going in such a hurry, man?" It was the bearded one.

I didn't answer. I was afraid my voice would crack. I didn't want them to smell the fear in me.

"You know, man, we don't like pig informers around here."

"Who said I was an informer?"

"Now see there, fellas, he's getting smart with me. You heard that didn't you, fellas? Now smart guy, you know you shouldn't get smart with people, you know, 'cause like other people can get their feelings hurt real easy, you know that, man?"

137

The others were smiling. One of the beard's group was really getting turned on by the whole scene, and kept nudging his friend and snickering.

"Answer me, man. What's the matter with you? Can't you fucking talk?"

I didn't say anything. I knew it wouldn't help. They were after blood and that was that. The beard turned toward the others.

"You see that, fellas? Impolite, too. No fucking manners. Okay, Mr. Smart-guy-pig-informer, I'm going to give you a lesson in manners. I think you need to learn some manners."

He reached into his pants pocket and pulled out a dog chain. The one behind him squealed in delight. The beard doubled up the chain and let it dangle down at his side. Then he started forward. I stood frozen to the ground, almost hypnotized with terror, watching the chain catch the light as it swung slowly back and forth. It was now or never. I aimed the kick directly at his crotch. The chain flew out of his hand and he screamed in agony and fell. The others had been stunned by his scream just long enough for me to spin around and start running. I grazed a blow off the head of one of the sidewalk commandos as I ran forward and knocked him off balance into the alley wall. I charged down the alley and pulled a trash can over as I went by and heard one of them crash into it and swear loudly as he fell.

I ran out of the alley and sailed across Melrose. The light was against me and the deafening din of car horns blared in my ears as cars slammed on their brakes and swerved to miss me, but I kept on running. I made it to the other side and sprinted down a small side street that ran into a residential area. I could hear their footsteps behind me getting louder and I put on every bit of speed I could muster, but I was starting to get winded. I thought I could hear them grunting behind me, but I couldn't be sure if that was them or me. I ran up to the end of the block, turned the corner, and ran up the first driveway. At the top of the driveway, I scaled a low wooden fence and dropped into the backyard. I crouched down, trying to hold my breath, and listened.

Their footsteps grew confused and I heard one of them say, "Maybe he went in here," and then I heard one of them coming up the driveway, cautiously. He stopped on the other side of the fence. I could hear him breathing. He waited there for a few seconds, listening to the darkness for some sign. I felt as if I were balancing on the edge of a razor blade, trying to hold my breath, my lungs threatening to burst, then I heard him start to move back down the driveway and I took a breath. Safe. Jesus.

The back door of the house opened and an old man stuck his head out and peered into the backyard. "Who's there?"

"He's in here!" the voice called from the driveway.

I took off across the yard.

"Hey, you!" the old man called as I trampled his flower bed and scrambled up a brick wall. I dropped on all fours into an alley and I heard the old man yelling at the leather jackets who were trampling his flowers. I ran across the alley, climbed another wooden fence, dropped into another backyard, ran through to another street, ran up a half block to another alley, went down to the next street and jumped into somebody's front yard bushes. I couldn't move another step. My chest had a knife in it and there was no more air left in my body to make my muscles obey. I looked down at my hands. They were bleeding. I sat there sweating, wedged in between the bushes and the front wall of the house. Somewhere in the house a dog was barking, but I didn't care; all I cared about was oxygen.

To hell with it. If they find me, they find me.

But nobody came.

I waited for about ten minutes before I moved out of the

yard and started to make my way back toward Melrose. I kept to the alleys the whole way, my senses alert to the slightest sound. My car was still parked in the same place —untouched—and there was no sign of the leather boys. I got in it and got out of there as fast as I could.

I saw a coffee shop and suddenly felt ravenously hungry, so I pulled in. I must have looked nice because everybody in the place turned around and stared when I came in. I ordered a sandwich and some coffee and leaned my head back on the soft back of the booth and closed my eyes. Then I felt it start to rise in me. That sonofabitch had nearly gotten me killed. By the time the sandwich came, the rage had completely taken over my body and I wolfed down the food, paid the check, and left.

The Porsche was in the driveway and all the lights in the house were on when I drove up. I got the tire iron out of the car and walked up to the front door. When I got to the front porch I stopped and listened. Everything was still. Too still. A cool breeze blew from somewhere up the street and chilled the back of my neck. There was something wrong inside, I could feel it. Something very, very wrong.

The door moved freely on its hinges, letting a crack of light from inside splash onto my shoes. I stepped back out of the light. The tiny hairs at the back of my neck were tingling now, my body giving me the message that I was not going to like what I was going to find inside. I asked myself what the hell I was doing here, why didn't I go home and call the police, and let them handle it. But then I always asked myself that question and it never seemed to do any good. I reached out and pushed the door open slowly with my left hand.

"Ruane?"

No answer.

"Ruane?"

I peered through the hinged crack in the door to make

sure there was nobody standing behind it, and stepped into the hallway. The entrance hall was empty. I stepped softly across the carpet to the living room steps, and stopped there, listening. Not a sound.

There was nobody in the living room, either, although there was plenty of evidence that somebody had been there. The place looked like Mighty Joe Young's rumpus room. All the pillows on the couch and the chairs had been split, the stuffing strewn all over the carpet. The china cabinet was open and emptied of its contents. A large, ominous, red stain had settled and dried in the carpet.

In the bedroom the scene was pretty much the same. The closets had been ransacked, bureau drawers pulled out and clothes thrown about everywhere; the mattress was off the bed and the box springs had been slashed. But whoever had redecorated the rest of the house had decided to polish off this room by leaving a striking piece of furniture. What alive had been Christopher Ruane was wedged down between the bed and the wall. He was dressed in what I had seen him in in the Trojan Horse except for the three blackened holes that had soaked the front of his shirt with blood. His eyes, glazed and slightly crossed, stared listlessly up at the ceiling. Blood was smeared along the wall in back of him in five parallel streaks, apparently where he had tried to get up and failed.

I bent down and felt for a pulse at the throat. There was none, but the skin was still warm. I took a closer look at the bullet holes in his shirt. Whoever had done it had gotten pretty close, judging by the powder tattoos.

After searching the rest of the house, I went into the kitchen, making a lot of noise tiptoeing over the shelves of broken dishes. The back door was open and I stepped out onto the back porch, ducking my head to miss a clothesline.

It was a fine night, and I thought it was funny that I hadn't noticed it until now. The stars were visible through the

141

smog canopy and crickets sang from their cozy homes in the bushes, oblivious to the fact that the owner of the property on which they sat chirping was inside dead with three bullet holes in his body.

The old wooden gate in the fence that enclosed the tiny backyard stood wide open. I walked to it and stepped out into the alley. A bent and battered trash can lay on its side in the middle of the alley and across the way, several gray cement bricks, apparently from the hole that had been knocked in the opposite wall, were lying broken on the pavement. A dog barked somewhere in another yard. I went back inside and called the police.

I was relaxing on the couch in the living room when they arrived.

"You're the one that called in about a murder?" the first patrolman asked sharply.

I nodded. "In there," I said, pointing to the bedroom.

The man's partner went into the bedroom. He came out, nodded to the other one who went back outside to call Homicide, and came over to the couch.

"Let's have some identification."

He looked at my driver's license, pulled it out of its plastic case, and leafed through the rest of the wallet. "Private detective, huh?"

I nodded. The other cop came back inside and the three of us waited for Homicide to arrive.

The detectives who came later introduced themselves as Graffton and Fuchs. They questioned me while in the bedroom the medical examiner examined and the photographer photographed and the measuring man taped off the room, calling out the dimensions to a sketcher, who on a piece of lined graph paper filled in the numbers on the drawing he had made. In the living room where we were sitting, an evidence man had found the stain on the rug and was humming while he was working on it. He scraped a bit of the stain onto a piece of filter paper, then filled a test tube which he brought out of his satchel with distilled water, added benzidine dihydrochloride and about one c.c. of hydrogen peroxide, and shook it up. With an eyedropper, he carefully placed a drop of the solution on the paper. It turned a bright blue-green. It was blood.

The faces of Graffton and Fuchs were expressionless, anesthetized by having answered too many three-o-clock-in-the-morning calls like this one. Neither of them looked too pleased at the thought of being here.

I took it for granted that Fuchs was the investigator in charge, for he was asking the questions, while Graffton sat sucking on a pipe, taking down my answers. The pipe tobacco was sweet and thick, and it lulled me into a false sense of well-being. I would have had no trouble going to sleep right there in that chair if they would have let me, but I could see by the look on Fuchs' face that he wasn't going to let me. They were both looking at me, so I felt compelled to say something.

"I have called you all together, dearly beloved. . . ."

Fuchs's face darkened and he leaned forward. "What?"

I could have gone on, but I thought better of it. There are lots of guys who love to get smart with cops. I'm not one of them. I've watched a couple of those cuties get their hands accidentally caught in slamming squad car doors when there was nobody around to appreciate their scintillating wit. Rules to live by—never look for trouble when all it can buy you is more trouble. "Nothing."

"What?"

I waved my hand in the air and looked away. "Nothing."

He seemed content to let that one ride and leaned back in his chair. "You knew the victim, right?"

"Look, sergeant, I'm tired. We've been through all this already. I'd like to go home."

"Mister, see these bags under my eyes? I'm tired too.

We're all tired. Everybody in this room would like to go home. But we won't until we're finished here. We'll go through it again and then maybe a few more times until I say it's time to quit. So just answer the questions."

"I didn't say I knew him. I said I'd met him several times."

"How?"

"I'm working for an attorney, Paul Ellman. Ruane's name came up during an investigation I was making and I came here a couple of times in the past week to question him."

"About what?"

"His possible involvement with our case."

"Which is?"

"The Warren murders."

Graffton looked up from his notepad with mild interest, the face softening for an instant before springing back into its original cast.

"And just what was the victim's involvement with your case?"

The victim. The victim. It was always the victim. I don't know why it bothered me so much, but it did. Probably because it made me think how tenuous identities really are, including my own. One minute, Christopher Ruane, Jacob Asch. Then, with a flick of a wrist, a little tension on an index finger, no face, no name, nothing. Merely the victim.

"What was the victim's involvement with your case?" he repeated, a little louder.

"Possibly none. I hadn't found anything specific."

"Then why did you bother to question him more than once?"

"You've got trained ears, sergeant; they pick up everything. Ruane was in a car accident with Sheila Warren last year. He was a passenger in her car. He told me he'd met her only once, that night. He was lying."

144

"How do you know?"

"Because he said he picked her up at the Key Club in Beverly Hills and went with her because he thought she would be a hot piece of ass."

"What's so strange about that?"

"Ruane was gay."

"How do you know?"

"I know, believe me. He liked leather boys. As a matter of fact, a couple of his friends tried to beat the shit out of me tonight at a place called the Trojan Horse. Ruane was there and told them I was a police informer."

Graffton adjusted the pipe in his mouth, and the wood made a clicking sound against his teeth. "Why would he do that?"

"Because he didn't like the questions I was asking him. Ruane was what you would call an uncooperative interviewee. He refused at first to acknowledge he even knew Sheila Warren. The second time he admitted he did and said he'd only denied it because he didn't want to get involved in a murder case, that he'd had enough trouble before."

"What kind of trouble?"

"Dope. He'd been busted on a dope charge a few months back and got off with a fine and a year's probation. He was dealing shit, but not bigtime." Graffton plucked the pipe out of his mouth, looked into the cold gray ashes in the bowl, started to put them into the ashtray on the table, thought better of it, and wound up tapping them into his hand and transferring them into his coat pocket.

The evidence man was over us now. He had a piece of paper filled with a fine white powder and a soft brush, and started dusting off the coffee table.

"When can I go home?"

"When we're through with you. We've got some more questions to ask you yet and it seems we're getting in the way here. I think we'd better go downtown."

I had a sudden vivid picture of this going on till dawn so I said to Fuchs, "Do me a favor."

"What?"

"Call Sergeant Albert Herrera, Sheriff's Homicide. He'll verify my story."

"We'll do that in a little while."

I went downtown in a squad car, one of the policemen following in my Plymouth. We sat over paper cups of bitter coffee and stale donuts, going over the same old questions over and over until seven a.m., when they finally got the hint that I didn't know much about Ruane, took a statement, and let me go.

When I got home, I called Al Herrera. He didn't sound overjoyed to hear my voice, but that didn't bother me. Overjoy is not one of the emotions I generally inspire in people.

"You could have at least held off until eight or nine o'clock to give those guys my name as a character reference. Those goddamn cops had the nerve to wake me up at home at five-thirty this morning to ask me if I knew a Jacob Asch."

"Sorry, Albert old boy. It couldn't be helped."

"What do they think about the murder?"

"They seem to think it was a fag killing. They think Ruane took the wrong guy home with him and the guy got overwhelmed with guilt and flipped out and killed him. That's what they think the tearing up of the house was— the guy going berserk and tearing up everything of Ruane's he could get his hands on."

"What do *you* think?"

"It could be the way they think. Whoever killed Ruane got close enough to leave powder burns on his shirt. But I don't think Ruane had time enough to pick up somebody and take him home and seduce him from the time I saw him in the Trojan Horse to the time I got over to the house."

"You think it might be tied in with the Warren thing?"

"I don't know. I'm going to try to find out."

"Well you do that, kid. Except the next time, find your bodies in the daytime. I need my beauty rest."

"I'll do that, Al. Thanks for the plug with Fuchs."

"Sure. Take it easy."

CHAPTER 16

With some effort and a Dexie I made it down to the office by noon. The mail was on the floor inside, where it had been pushed through the mail slot in the door. There was a letter from Union Oil and one from Master Charge, a tearsheet from Sav-Mor Markets that said I could get 13¢ off on any can of S&W prunes in their stores, and a perfumed letter from an Elaine Tibbett of 1302 Grenville Lane, Los Angeles. The perfumed letter smelled the most promising, so I opened it first.

Mrs. Tibbett turned out to be a seventy-four-year-old widow who explained in arthritic handwriting that she wanted me to help her find her lost poodle, Sadie. She said she had left $50,000 in her will to Sadie and now she (Sadie) was missing and she was afraid of having no heir. She said she was at her wits' end, and after reading her letter, so was I. I put the letter in my desk drawer and slit open the letters from Master Charge and Union Oil.

Both letters turned out to be the same—notifications that they were revoking my credit cards due to the fact that they had found me to be a bad credit risk. Bad credit risk, hell. It was true my bank balance seldom went above three figures, but neither of these companies had ever had to notify me that I was late with a payment. It was not unusual for a computer to make a mistake on billing; it happened all the time. But the chances that two computers at two different companies would make the same mistake at exactly the same time were quite a bit slimmer. It suddenly made sense why somebody would want to pay up the nose for a rundown, noisy house that for three years had been starving for tenants. Somebody was showing me how vulnerable I was, that I was now playing in the big leagues.

I looked up Anthony Gutierrez in the phone book and dialed the number.

"Hello?"

"Mr. Gutierrez, this is Jacob Asch."

"Yes, Mr. Asch. How are you?"

"Fine. Listen, Mr. Gutierrez, the man who rented your house from under me—what's his name?"

There was a hesitation.

"His name?"

"Yes, his name. I have a reason for asking."

"He said his name was James Jones."

"What did he look like?"

"Look like? Well, I don't know. You see, he handled everything over the phone."

"Over the phone?"

"That's right. He called me up and said his name was James Jones and he wanted to rent my house on Bufort Street for a year. Two days later, a cashier's check came in the mail for the first six months' rent."

"Was there an address with the check? On the envelope?"

"No, as I remember, it was a plain white envelope."

"Didn't you think that was a little unusual?"

"A little. But I learned a long time ago not to look a gift horse in the mouth." His voice became suddenly conciliatory. "Mr. Asch, you will be able to move your things out by the first, won't you? If not, perhaps I could arrange for a few days—"

149

"Don't worry, Mr. Gutierrez. I won't jeopardize your gift horse."

I hung up and was sitting there thinking when the phone rang. It was Ellman.

"Remember you asked me to check out Folsom's lawyer in that civil case over the camera equipment? Name was Matthies. Well, I got the stuff on him. He's a Beverly Hills attorney, all right, and it seems he's got only one client. A man by the name of Lewis T. Gorman. Owns a multimillion-dollar plastics manufacturing firm called International Synthetics."

"That's all you got?"

"What more do you want?"

"Nothing. I'll have him checked out. Thanks, Paul."

I called the editorial department of the *Chronicle* and asked for extension 405.

"Sangster speaking."

"Mike, this is Jake."

"Jake! How's the private eye biz? What's cooking?"

"Nothing much, Mike. Hey, I was wondering if you could do me a little favor. I need anything you've got in the morgue on a Lewis T. Gorman."

"Gorman, huh?"

"Know him?"

"Know of him. He throws some of the biggest society bashes in the city."

"Think you've got anything in the files on him?"

"Society should have plenty. I'll talk to Susie Amworth. She works in that section and she's a pretty good kid. Now that I think about it, she might have even covered one or two of his parties. How soon you need the info?"

"This afternoon."

"You don't give a guy a lot of time to work."

"I'll meet you at four at Nate's. I'll even buy you something to eat."

150

"In that case, I'll skip lunch."

"And get me anything you can, Mike—address, phone numbers, the works."

"Righto. Bye."

It was a little after four when I got to Nate's Deli and through the front window I could see Mike's gray head hunched over a sandwich. He looked up and waved. Through the window he looked as if he had put on weight, but when I got over to the booth I could see it was just an illusion created by the glass and the half a pastrami sandwich he had in his mouth. When he had chewed and swallowed, his face went back to its long, thin self. I slid into the booth and we shook hands.

"Goddamn, where you been keeping yourself? I haven't seen you in months."

"I've been around." The waitress came and I ordered coffee. Mike dug into his briefcase and pulled out three Xeroxed articles.

One was a silly little fashion piece on Gorman's fabulous wardrobe. In another, Gorman talked about his house which he had designed himself according to a new architectural concept he had dreamed up called "organic architecture"—structures designed as living systems—which he said was going to be the "wave of the future." The third was a clipping from the society section, dated April 2, 1971. It read:

Well, there was another party at Lewis T. Gorman's luxurious Malibu estate last night, and as usual, it was a whopper. Like all Gorman's affairs, from beginning to end, the party was run like a well-oiled machine, with the host completely taking charge of the show to make sure that the 600-odd guests had a good time.

The theme of the party was Carnival Time, and game booths were set up outside on the grounds, complete with

151

barkers. There, partygoers could attempt to knock over iron milk bottles with a baseball or try their luck at beating famous sleight-of-hand expert Jack Bailey at the old shell game.

Among more celebrated personalities at the party were the Edward Carpenters, the Robert Bishops, and actor Larry Majors and his date, pretty Sylvia Ritter.

But even the selection of the guests was run in a precise, scientific manner. Invitations were sent out according to the dictates of an IBM computer that Gorman keeps in his twenty-three-room mansion overlooking the Pacific. Personality profiles are filed on date cards and all of Gorman's guests are chosen according to the nature of the function, to insure that things run harmoniously. "The secret of a good party," the happy host said, "like the secret of anything, is order. Having the wrong people at the wrong function would be as disastrous as serving roast pork at a bar mitzvah."

Of course there are always crashers at the Gorman parties, and they are almost always admitted. Actress Jayne Murray was one last night. "I just had to come up to see what it was like," she said.

Jayne was not disappointed by the proceedings, but then how could you be disappointed by a party à la Gorman?

Alongside the article was a photograph of Gorman standing with another couple. He was wearing a dark velvet dinner jacket and a white dress shirt with lace cuffs and a ruffled front. He looked to be in his early forties and had dark hair and whatever good looks he might have had were spoiled by his eyes, which were small and much too close together.

"What's his story?"

"From what I could get, Gorman was apparently born and raised in New Jersey. His father was a chemist. I guess chemistry runs in the family strain, because Gorman was

152

supposedly a child genius with chemicals. He got a scholarship to Princeton at the age of sixteen and the Defense Department pulled him out of there to go to work for them. He worked for the government for a few years until the Samson Corporation—the big 'think tank' south of El Segundo—offered him a job. So he pulled up stakes and moved out to California. That was twelve years ago. He worked for them for two years until he invented Gormanite. The stuff is some sort of plastic used in missiles because of its resiliency and its resistance to high temperatures. Gorman started his own plant to manufacture the stuff—International Synthetics—and was a millionaire at thirty-two. Then he retired to his dream house in Malibu. He designed it himself and put everything in it anybody could want—indoor-outdoor swimming pools, tennis courts, sauna baths, gymnasium. He has special cooks on call twenty-four hours a day to prepare the dishes he likes. He even runs International Synthetics from there; he has an office completely staffed with secretaries, Telex machines, everything."

"Sounds like a pretty well-organized man."

"Well-organized isn't the word. The guy is weird city."

"Why?"

"For one thing, he's a goddamn hermit. Never leaves his house. Says he doesn't like to go out because he finds the world too chaotic. Says he has everything he wants at the house, so why leave? Anything he wants and doesn't have, he imports."

"Like people."

"Huh?"

I pointed to the article about the party.

"Oh yeah. Anyway, I talked to Susie Amworth who's been up to the house to interview Gorman. She says he's a nice guy, but very condescending. His work habits are really weird, too. She said he only conducts his business at

153

night, usually after midnight. He works all night and sleeps during the day."

"Just like Howard Hughes."

"Yeah. Or Count Dracula. What are you interested in Gorman for, anyway? What are you working on?"

When I told him I was working on the Warren murders, his eyes grew big. "You mean Gorman's got something to do with the Warren murders? Jesus Christ, Jake, fill me in."

"No, I don't mean Gorman's got anything to do with the Warren murders. His name just came up, that's all, and I'm checking him out. Purely routine."

"I've heard that line before."

"Maybe, but it's true. I can't tell you anything, Mike, or I would."

"Jake, this is your old buddy Mike. You can tell me, for chrissakes. Who was it that stuck up for you when old man Simon started bad-mouthing you to everybody in town and nearly got fired in the process?"

"How come every time you smell a story, you start dredging all that up? Look, Mike, I promise you I'll give you the exclusive if anything breaks. That's all I can tell you for now. But until I give you the word, I'm going to have to ask you to keep quiet about this and not ask me any more questions."

"That's an awful big request to ask of an old bloodhound like me."

"But it's one you'll keep."

He looked down at his empty plate and shoved it away from him. "Okay, we'll do it your way."

"How are things at the rag?"

"Same as usual. Oh, Thompson's leaving."

"Fired or quit?"

"Quit. The *Toronto Clarion* offered him the editor-in-chief job and he took it. He's leaving at the end of the month."

154

"The place should smell better at the end of the month, anyway. Who's taking over his spot?"

"Eddie Samuelson."

"Eddie's a good man. I always got along with Eddie."

"He asked about you the other day, as a matter of fact. Wanted to know how you were doing."

"Tell him peachy. I've got a missing poodle case coming up that's going to immortalize me. Just like Sherlock Holmes."

"Hmm?"

"Nothing."

"I think he had it in the back of his mind to offer you your old job back."

"If he wants to keep that promotion, that's where it had better stay—in the back of his mind."

"That's what he's afraid of, I think. He knows he'd be drawing fire from all sides. There sure are a lot of people over there who hate your guts for some strange reason."

"They're just jealous of my charm and good looks."

"And your big feet that always manage to step on somebody's toes."

"Well anyway, you can tell Eddie I don't need the *Chronicle*. I got an offer last month from the *San Gabriel Valley Sun*."

"You going to take it?"

"Hell, I'd rather be doing what I'm doing than work for the *San Gabriel Valley Sun*, and that's saying something. But it may be a sign that the ice is breaking up."

"Sure. It's just a matter of time."

"Did you get an address and phone number for me?"

"Huh?"

"For Gorman."

"Oh yeah." He reached into his briefcase and pulled out a piece of paper. On it was scrawled: *Lewis Gorman 39079 Summit View Rd., Malibu Phone 394-1421.*

It took a few seconds for the familiarity of that address to sink in, but it finally dawned on me where I'd seen it before. In the Registry of Voters as a former address for Christopher Ruane.

"Something wrong?"

"No," I said, "nothing." He would just start pumping me with more questions I wouldn't be able to answer. He'd get his story soon enough, if there was one.

"He's having another one Thursday, by the way."

"Who's having another what?"

"Gorman. He's having another party on Thursday."

I folded the paper up and put it in my pocket. "You think you could get me a press pass into that party, Mike?"

"I was afraid you were going to ask that."

"You'd be doing both of us a favor. If Gorman's mixed up in anything, I'm not going to find it out sitting here. You want your story? Get me a press pass."

"All right. I'll see what I can do, on one condition."

"What's that?"

"I go along."

"Fair enough. I'll call you tomorrow."

His eyes sparkled at me. "I'll talk to Susie. She knows Gorman and she can leave word that we'll be coming up on Thursday to cover the party for the *Chronicle*. Shouldn't be any problem. Gorman takes pride in his parties and loves publicity on them."

I slid out of the booth and picked up the food check on the table. "It'll be just like old times."

"Yeah, except instead of covering a murder, we'll be covering a catered affair for the *haut monde*. Thrilling."

I left Mike and drove back across town toward Bel Air. When I got to Beverly Hills, I stopped at a phone booth in a gas station and called Gloria Pilsen. I expected to have to wrestle linguistically with the Mexican maid, but was pleasantly surprised to hear Gloria's voice answer the ring.

156

"Gloria?"

"Who's this?"

"Jake Asch."

"Jacob daaarling. I'm starting to believe all this psychic nonsense. I was just thinking about you. How's that for ESP?"

"Not bad."

"You've decided to take me up on my offer of a martini, or marriage?"

"The martini will do for starters. We can see about the marriage later."

"You're a slow courter, dear."

"Yeah, but I might give in sooner than you think. I'm getting tired of working for a living. I'd also like to ask you a few more questions, if you don't mind."

"You're a horrible man—did you know that? What happens when this old information pump runs dry? You'll just abandon me, like a business venture that's no longer profitable. Ah, well, we must make do, I suppose. Where are you?"

"In a gas station about ten minutes away. I'm leaving now."

I stepped out of the booth and scanned the street. The white Ford was across the street in another gas station, and the man with the round face was at the Coke machine, drinking a soda. When he saw me crossing the street, he hurriedly drained the soda, stuck the empty into the wire rack, and got back in his car. He seemed slightly jittery when I came up alongside the car and leaned on the window.

"How's Whittaker?"

He tried to look confused, but didn't do a very good job of it. "Whittaker? Whittaker who?"

"Here we go again. Okay, we'll play the game. Brian Whittaker, the lawyer. Now it's your turn to say, 'I'm afraid you've made some mistake, I don't know any Brian Whittaker.' "

"I'm afraid you've made some mistake. I don't know any Brian Whittaker."

I reached in and pulled his keys out of the ignition. "Now let's be reasonable, shall we? I don't particularly mind your tailing me, but I'd like to know your name and who's hired you to do it and why."

"You must be crazy. Give me back my keys."

"I might be crazy, buddy, but in about two seconds you're going to be walking."

The man looked anxiously at the keys that were dangling from my fingers and licked his lips. He made a lunge for them, but I pulled my hand back and he missed. He jerked on the door handle and tried to step out, but I kicked the door closed and he pulled his foot inside just in time. He didn't seem to want to make another move to open it.

"Come on, man, have a heart. We're both in the same line of work. Give me back my keys."

"Answers first."

"Okay, okay. My name is Harvey Cox. I work for the Bellson Investigation Agency." He showed me his identification.

"Why are you following me?"

"I don't know. This guy Whittaker comes into the agency and says he wants you followed and wants a report on all your movements. That's all I know."

"You're sure that's all you know?"

"Really, that's all. They didn't tell me anything more than that."

"Well, Harvey, I'm going to give you a lesson in detective work right now. If you can find these, you can find anything."

I threw the keys into a hedge that ran alongside the gas station.

"Ahhhhh, Christ. What in the hell did you do that for?"

"I've taken you on as my protégé, Harvey old boy. Lesson number one—always carry a spare set of car keys. Oh—and I wouldn't want you to lose your job, so I'll tell you where I'm going now. The residence of Mrs. Gloria Pilsen, 904 Lambretta Drive, Bel Air. I should be there for about half an hour. After that, I'll be home."

As I crossed the street, he was down on all fours, sweating and swearing, digging in the hedge, while the gas station attendant yelled at him to move his car and he yelled back that if the sonofabitch wanted the car moved, he could goddamn help him look for his keys.

Gloria answered the doorbell, and welcomed me with a kiss on the cheek. "Come in, darling. There's somebody here who's anxious to meet you."

I followed her into the living room. Standing by the fireplace was a short man with hair the color of a case of snowblindness. He was stout and conservatively dressed in a gray wool suit which looked as if it might have been warm for the weather outside. The mouth was thin and ascetic and slightly turned up at the edges in a perpetual mock smile. Crocodiles smiled like that.

He left the fireplace and moved over to stand in back of a chair and I noticed there was an economy in the way he moved. I judged he would probably use his words the same way—sparingly, without waste.

"Jacob Asch, my father, Henry Toppinger."

He gave me a dissecting look that peeled away my flesh and left me bone-naked. He didn't offer his hand.

"You'll have to excuse Daddy. He's a self-made man. And since the self he's made comes to somewhere around twenty million dollars, he's decided he can dispense with the bothersome little formalities of protocol."

The man looked at his daughter solemnly, then back at me.

159

"So you're the man who won't take bribes from my 'messenger boys'?"

"That's right. Are you the man who's renting my house?"

"What?"

"Whom do you know at Union Oil, Mr. Toppinger?"

The confusion that was planted firmly on his face looked real.

Gloria stepped in between us, holding up her hands. "Before you two touch gloves and come out fighting, would you like a drink, Jacob? Nobody is going to accuse me of being a rotten hostess just because my father is an ill-mannered boor."

"Thanks. Bourbon on the rocks, please."

She moved away and came back with a drink. "Don't feel conspicuous if Daddy stares at the drink in your hand—he's trying to. He has no vices like the rest of us. Doesn't drink, doesn't smoke—the last of the red-hot Puritans. Sheila and Jimmy and I were the results of only three minutes of weakness out of an otherwise totally moral life."

"Shut up, Gloria," he said with no apparent malice. Maybe he was used to it. "I didn't leave my businesses to fly out here to beat around the bush, Asch. Here—"

He reached inside his breast pocket, pulled out an envelope and threw it down on the table in front of me. I picked it up and opened the flap. Inside was a piece of eight mm filmstrip. I held it up against the light of the french windows that opened onto the patio. On the three frames Sheila Warren lay on a carpet, in a very compromising position. She was naked except for a pair of black nylon stockings, some spiked high heels, and a black garter belt. The envelope was postmarked Los Angeles.

"Who sent you this?"

"I don't know. It arrived at my office in Pittsburgh registered mail a week ago. It was obviously sent by somebody who knew I was in Pittsburgh."

"Was there a note? Anything with the film strip?"

"Yes. This."

He pulled a piece of paper out of his pocket and handed it to me. It was a note, the letters of which had been clipped from magazines and pasted together.

ThiS Is jUST A sAmpLE. MorE to COme.

"Were you contacted again?"

"No."

"Have you shown this note to the police?"

"Of course not. Do you think I want my name splattered across every newspaper in the country?"

"The police usually handle these matters with the utmost care."

He looked at me as if I were a lunatic who'd just jumped the wall at Camarillo. "The police are publicity-crazy opportunists who would sell out their own mothers to get their names in the papers."

"What are you showing me all this for?"

"I made a mistake sending Whittaker. I realize that now. I misjudged the animal I was dealing with. In business, that can be a fatal mistake, but that's the price you pay working through third parties. You can't get the feeling of the man. I thought five thousand would be enough, but apparently it isn't. How much?"

"How much what?"

"Damn it, let's not play games. I detest games. How much money do you want for those films?"

"I don't have them."

"When you get your hands on them."

"I may never get my hands on them."

"*If* you find them, then."

"You know, I must be the best private detective in the

world. Everybody wants to hire me. The only trouble is, everybody wants to hire me for the same job. I'm beginning to feel like a piece of furniture at an auction. I've already gone through all this with your lawyer, Mr. Toppinger. I'm already employed. My client's case may depend on those films and I can't turn them over to whoever offers me the most money for them. There's a matter of ethics involved. As a businessman you can surely—"

"Damn ethics!" he thundered. "I didn't get to where I am today because of ethics. I got here from making the right moves and making them first. Damn ethics. My daughter's reputation is at stake."

"You mean *your* reputation is at stake. Your daughter is dead, mister, and a corpse doesn't have a reputation. All it's got is a little tag on its big toe that tells the pathologist down at the morgue what freezer box it goes in."

His face turned scarlet, and his nails dug into the back of the chair. "You insolent son of a bitch, don't you ever talk to me like that!"

I finished off my drink and set the glass down on the table. "You know, Toppinger, I'm not so sure you didn't have your own daughter killed. If the shit ever hit the fan, she could have been quite an embarrassment to you socially. Actually her being murdered when she was might have saved you some scandal."

A large vein bulged and twitched in the middle of his forehead. "Get out, you filthy bastard. GET OUT!"

I smiled and turned to Gloria, who was amusedly watching the fireworks. "Can I talk to you for a minute?"

She put her drink down and excused herself and the two of us started for the door. When we reached the end of the living room, I turned back to Toppinger. "Oh, and Mr. Toppinger, before I forget: your boy Whittaker has hired another investigator to follow me. I don't work well with a tail. Tell him to get rid of him, otherwise those films you're so worried about might never turn up even if they do, if you know what I mean."

As soon as we got out the front door, Gloria broke out laughing and fell on my arm. "Nobody has ever talked like that to my father. I wish I had *that* on film. His face! The most beautiful color red I've ever seen. Like a sunset in Morocco."

"Did you know about your sister's being on those films?"

"Today was the first I'd heard of it."

"You're sure?"

"Sure I'm sure. Why would I lie?"

"For protection."

"Protection from what? I could care less if my sister made her film debut in every nudie theatre in L.A. If it would make my father turn that lovely shade of red, I'd distribute them myself."

"There's no love lost between you two, is there?"

"You can't lose something you never had. The only things my father ever loved were his blessed financial empire and Sheila. I suppose that was why he arranged to have us kids split up the way we were."

"What do you mean 'arranged?' "

"Just what I said. He arranged the settlement of custody just like he arranges everything else—with money. He bribed my mother to agree to the separation and she did."

"Where is your mother now?"

"Dead. She was a lush, and one night she got drunk and fell down and hit her head and died. And I was glad when she did. Her drinking bouts used to terrify me as a kid. I hated her and I never forgave my father for abandoning me to her the way he did."

I decided to pass on any further discussions of the Top-

163

pinger family squabbles. "Ever heard of a man by the name of Lewis Gorman?"

Her eyes searched mine. "I know Lewis casually. I've been to a couple of his parties."

"What's he like?"

"Why do you ask?"

"Just curious."

"Charming, highly intelligent, well-versed in almost every subject. Completely devoid of a sense of humor. He's very introverted, but in some ways very forward. That's a paradox, isn't it?"

"It could be, I suppose. It depends on what you mean by forward. He ever try to make a pass at you?"

"Hardly. Lewis is queer as hell."

"How do you know?"

"Let's just say that there have been a few unrepeatable incidents involving a couple of people I know."

"Who?"

"I couldn't possibly tell you that, love, even being as sexy as you are. You'll just have to take my word for it."

"I guess so. Thanks for the drink. If your father gets another note, let me know."

"When are we going to get together again? I've called you several times. You're never in."

"I've been busy."

"I'll be free tonight. Why don't you come by?"

"I've got to get some sleep tonight or I'll drop."

"A likely story."

"But a true one. I've been averaging about four hours a night since I started on this case. To handle you, I have to be rested. I'll tell you what—I'll be over the night I crack this case and we'll have a hell of a time. How's that?"

"Terrible. But I guess it will have to do."

I headed down the driveway and when I hit the street, I looked around for a white Ford. The street was deserted and I hit the gas, figuring that I must have given those keys a pretty good toss after all.

CHAPTER 17

The light turned green and as Mike and I took off, I tried to pinpoint exactly what in my own mind was drawing me down the Pacific Coast Highway toward the Malibu mountains and Lewis T. Gorman. There was, of course, a little matter of a known homosexual who had been caught dealing and who knew Sheila Warren and who had a same former address as Gorman, another reputed homosexual, and who had been mysteriously shot to death with a .32 caliber pistol. But that wasn't all of it. There was something else, some unconscious, instinctual force that had a ring in my nose and was pulling me along, and *that* was what was bothering me. I never did believe in playing hunches, but that was what I was doing.

I stared out the window at the tiny boat lights flickering like dying stars far out on the endless black expanse of ocean. My thoughts were broken by Mike's voice.

"This the road here?"

"Yeah, that's it."

The road he pointed out was a winding, narrow road that rose sharply from the highway into the green hills above Malibu. We turned off and headed up it. About a quarter of a mile up the hill, we hit the cars. They were parked bumper-to-bumper on both sides of the street—Lincolns, Cadillacs, Ferraris, nothing older than a '72.

"Looks like there might be a party going on," Mike said. "Jesus Christ, I guess he invited a few people. Look at the cars."

166

After another quarter mile or so, on our left, the wall started. It was a high flagstone wall with broken glass imbedded in its top. It ran up the hill to the end of the road, which dead-ended in a sandy embankment, and next to the sandy embankment were the black iron gates which marked the entrance to the Gorman estate. As we drove through the gates, I noticed two closed-circuit television cameras mounted in the flagstone pillars on either side of us.

The house was well lighted and set well back from the road at the end of a long driveway. From what I could see, it was sitting on the edge of a cliff that overlooked the coast highway and the sea beyond. It was a modernistic structure, huge and white and rambling, and there was something about its geometry that set me ill at ease. None of its angles were right, none of its lines straight. The corners seemed to dissolve into one another, giving the impression that the house was alive and moving, some blind, repulsive, white slug clinging to a moist rock. The only thing that gave the house weight, that kept it from slithering away silently into the night, was the huge dome that rose from its center.

We pulled up in front and one of the uniformed parking valets opened the car door and scribbled down the license number on a ticket and handed it to Mike. We went down the flagstone walk to the thick oak front doors and went in. We were greeted by a flashbulb bursting in our eyes. A slim-legged girl in velvet hotpants put the Polaroid down on the table, counted off the seconds and peeled off the print.

"Name, please?"

"Jacob Billings."

She thumbed through the cards on a little filing box on the table. "Oh, yes, here it is. You're with the *Chronicle*, is that right, Mr. Billings?"

"Yes."

"May I see your press pass, please?"

I handed her my pass, she looked it over, and handed it back to me with a little white card. "Please fill this out."

The card wanted my name, sex, address, phone number, date of birth, and occupation. I filled in all the spaces, ad libbing here and there. When I was finished, she stapled the photograph to the card and put it on a pile on the table. Then she went through the same procedure with Mike.

"Just what's all that for?" I asked, pointing to the stack of cards.

The girl looked up. "Mr. Gorman requires it of all new guests. The information will be transferred to a computer programming card and stored for Mr. Gorman's future reference. Now, gentlemen, there is a buffet out by the pool. Drinks are being served at the bars located inside and outside on the grounds. Entertainment is being provided outside by the tennis courts. Thank you for coming. I hope you enjoy the party."

Someone else was coming in behind us. The girl reached over and picked up the Polaroid.

"What a robot," Mike whispered as we moved away. "I've seen warmer adding machines."

I nodded, but was too busy looking over the living room to answer. It was a gigantic circle built around a Swedish fireplace that blazed merrily from its couch-lined sunken pit. A huge copper chimney rose over the pit to the ceiling, twenty-five feet above. The ceiling was the inside of the dome.

The furniture was all low-slung modern blibs and blobs, and everything in the room, from the rug to the walls to the ceiling, was stark white. Hanging around the room were various paintings out of which I recognized a Chagall, a DeKooning, and a Matisse lithograph.

As immense as it was, the living room was already wall-to-wall people when we came in. The assortment of faces and shapes in the dinner-jacketed, backless, sleeveless, midied-maxied, seminude and glitteringly bejeweled crowd was varied, but I could feel a thickly omnipresent, unspoken bond holding the whole affair together—money. If a mad bomber chose to hit this house tonight, a lot of lawyers would clean up on estate settlements tomorrow and a lot of cash would pass on to anxiously waiting offspring. A whole new generation of inherited fortunes would rise up like a phoenix from the ashes of death and soar to the dizzying heights of moneydom.

We bumped and wedged and smiled and helloed our way through the mass of bodies that filled the room, finally making it to the bar.

"Ever feel out of place?" Mike asked. "Whiskey sour, please."

"I know what you mean. Bourbon and water. Don't worry about it. Let's go get something to eat."

We grabbed our drinks and made our way through the sliding glass doors that opened onto the grounds. A table arrangement twenty feet long sat by the pool. On it was displayed every imaginable dish to satisfy growling stomachs and fussy palates. Behind the tables, five cooks stood carving and ladling and dishing up and forking food onto the plates of guests who had lined up for the repast. We grabbed two plates and fell into line. After filling the plates with everything they could hold, we wandered over past a lighted fountain around the edge of which sat grotesque cement gargoyles which watched us with cold gray eyes. A five-piece band had set up their instruments on the tennis court and were moving into a Latin number. One lonely elderly couple, swaying to the rhythms, shuffled across the cement floor.

We walked over the grass to a stone bench and sat down. We ate in a gluttonous silence, watching people meander over the grounds and listening to the echoes of the music and laughter reverberate across the lawn.

A harsh female voice pierced the soft sounds of the party. "Mr. Gorman, telephone . . . Mr. Gorman, telephone . . ."

I turned around and saw that the voice was coming from a speaker box which was attached to a pepper tree behind us.

Mike looked around him. "This place reminds me of something from *1984*. Big Brother is watching you. Secretaries at the front door filing you away on little computer cards, speakers in the trees. You think there are television cameras in the bushes?"

"I don't know about the bushes, but there are a couple out by the front gate. We passed them when we drove in. Let's go see if we can find Mr. Gorman."

We went back toward the house. By the edge of the cliff, a girl in her mid-twenties, dressed in a scanty yellow dress, was sitting in a swing and was being pushed by her boyfriend out over the edge of the cliff. She was laughing, obviously pleased by the small crowd of onlookers who had gathered to watch. I walked to the edge and looked over. It was a good sixty-foot drop. It takes all kinds to make a party.

We wandered around for about twenty minutes and after making a few inquiries, managed to locate Gorman, who was standing by the fireplace surrounded by five or six couples. He was thin and immaculately dressed in an expertly tailored black dinner suit with velvet trim lapels and a black velvet bowtie. His hair was curly and red-brown, and he looked just like his picture, except for the eyes. They were small and too close together, like in the picture, but contained a concentrated energy that didn't photograph. Gorman was clearly dominating the conversation of the group, talking rapidly in a high-pitched nasal voice while the tiny dark eyes scanned the crowd of listeners intently, gauging every reaction to what he was saying. We moved to the fringe of the little group.

"When Fallon decided to give up the patronage of Santanelli, he fell from grace. He died as an artist."

"On the contrary," the silver-haired man standing next to him said, "I think some of his latest work is the best he's ever done."

"Yes? Name one."

"'Paris Street,' for example. That was done just last year."

"Yes, it was done last year. And it was a banal piece of trash."

"That is a matter of opinion."

Gorman raised one of his hands and waved it in the air. It was delicately tapered and pale and on one of the meticulously manicured fingers, was a black star sapphire ring about the size of a charcoal briquette. "No, that is precisely what it is not. The myth that art is purely subjective and not prone to objective analysis is a fallacy."

"And who is to be the judge of whether a piece of art is objectively good or bad?" a woman in a backless evening dress chimed in.

"The judge who is most objectively qualified for the task."

"That doesn't answer my question."

"Oh, but it does. There are those who are endowed with objectively superior taste and who are therefore the most qualified judges. They merely have to be found."

"And all must submit to their opinions?"

"Within their sphere of dominance."

"That sounds like elitism, Mr. Gorman."

He smiled faintly. "Are you denying that there is an elite? Let's not be naïve. There are people who are superior and there are people who are inferior. The former rule the latter. It has always been that way and it will always be that way, no matter what social theories you may wish to expound to sugar-coat the fact."

I decided I didn't like this Gorman, and it wasn't just because of the patronizing, condescending pose he presented, although that could have had something to do with it. It was more in the realm of an instant clashing of body chemicals.

The woman in the backless dress had opened her mouth again to interject something, but Gorman turned his attention suddenly away from her, cutting her off. "If you will excuse me, I must be attending to my other guests."

He bowed and turned and I leaned a little forward so I would bump shoulders when he passed. A little of my drink spilled out of my glass and onto the carpet.

"I'm terribly sorry. I seem to have soiled your beautiful carpet."

"Don't think a thing of it. My own clumsy fault." The dark eyes looked at me and smiled. There was something in them that made me feel uncomfortable, as if he recognized me, but I shook that feeling off. "I don't believe I've had the pleasure. I'm Lewis Gorman."

"Jacob Billings. I'm here to cover your party for the *Chronicle*. This is Mike Sangster, also of the *Chronicle*."

"Ah, yes, Susie Amworth called and said you two would be coming up," he said, shaking hands. The hand was cold and full of small, sharp bones.

"Fantastic house you have here, Mr. Gorman. I'm interested in architecture myself. Sort of a sideline. I read your article on organic architecture in the *Chronicle* and found it fascinating."

"This house was organically designed, you know. It functions similarly to a biological system. It's been refined since I was interviewed for that article. The bodily functions of the house—sight, hearing, communications, and other motor functions—are controlled from the Control Center, or brain, which is in the east wing, over that way. There are also three new auxiliary control centers, in separate areas

172

of the house, from which more local functions can be carried out—paging, regulation of lighting and temperature, security surveillance, things of that nature."

"That's really incredible. Someday I'd like to do a piece on your house for the paper."

"Fine. Talk to my secretary, Miss Schroeder, before you leave tonight and she'll schedule an appointment. I'd be glad to give you an interview. Now, if you'll forgive me—"

He turned sharply and snapped his fingers at the Filipino houseboy who was poised by the bar with a tray in his hands, and pointed to the rug where I'd spilled the drink. The Filipino, who apparently understood the signal, put the tray down and rushed over with a damp rag and began to wipe at the stain diligently. Mike and I moved away. Gorman was making his way across the room, smiling, greeting people, shaking hands, occasionally stopping for a quick conversation or to issue a command to a waiter or maid.

"What do you think?"

"I don't know," Mike said. "Something about him gives me the creeps."

"He sure has the routine down pat."

"Too pat. He's a goddamn machine. But he sure did seem to warm up to you."

"It seemed that way, didn't it? From what you told me, he's not that accessible to interviewers."

"He's not supposed to be. But maybe he's just proud of his house and wants a chance to show it off."

"Maybe."

We went over to the bar and ordered two more drinks.

"You stay here. I'll be back in a few minutes."

His head jerked up. "Where are you going?"

"Snooping. I want to see if I can get the layout of this place. If I'm not back in twenty minutes, send a search party after me."

I asked the bartender where the bathroom was and he pointed down the hallway that ran off the living room to my left. I thanked him and went down the hall. Paintings hung on the walls and I walked slowly down the hall, pretending to look at them. At the end of the hallway, on the right, was a set of double doors and opposite them was an open archway and a flight of carpeted stairs which led down to a heavy steel door. I went down the stairs and tried the door, but it was locked. I went back up into the hallway and tried the double doors. They weren't locked, so I went in.

I was in a large office with a high ceiling. A great steel desk was elevated on a platform in the middle of the room, insuring whoever sat behind it a clear view of anybody below and the four television screens mounted on the opposite wall. On the screens, guests moved through various parts of the house. I could see Mike on one of them, still standing by the bar. I waved to him and went back to business.

Most of the walls were taken up by shelves filled by thousands of thick volumes. In one corner a large IBM computer dozed peacefully. By the computer was another set of double doors and on them a large sign declared in stark red letters: PRIVATE—KEEP OUT.

I tried all the desk drawers, found them locked, and moved on to the marked doors. They were locked, too, so I pulled out my plastic lock-picking card out of my wallet, inserted it into the crack, and worked it until the handle turned freely in my hand.

When I let the door close behind me, I found I was in the dark. Then my pupils began to adjust and I could see I was at the top of a long flight of stairs that led downward. There were no visible lighting fixtures along the stairway, but the walls seemed to give off a faintly luminous light of their own. I followed the stairs down to the bottom, where they deadended into a door. I got out my card again and went to work.

The room beyond was small and barren, except for a few wooden crates that were lying around on the floor. The lighting was the same as the stairway outside and the walls threw off a dim, luminous, blue glow. It looked like a small storage room of some sort.

I went over to one of the crates, opened the lid, and started digging through the contents. I came up with leather thongs, a bamboo-handled cat-o'-nine tails, assorted pairs of handcuffs, leather strap gags and several strange-looking black leather face masks. In one of the other boxes were coils of nylon rope and maybe a dozen leather dildos, complete with harnesses. Another was filled with long black robes and when I dug down farther in that one, I found a wooden staff with an elaborately carved skull mounted on top. At the bottom, my hand hit something heavy and cold. Metal. I pulled up a brass candleholder shaped like a king cobra. It had its hood flared and looked like it was ready to strike.

I buried it beneath the robes again and made my exit. I went back up the stairs to the door and grabbed the handle. It didn't respond to my touch. Frozen. I took out my card and bent down eye-level to the handle. Then I noticed for the first time that the door had a metal lip on the inside. One way in, no way out. I'd seen this in Flash Gordon serials before. Now the floodgates would open and the passageway would fill up with water and I would drown like a rat. Shit! Jacob Asch caught with his pants down again.

I was wondering what to do, when I heard voices on the other side of the door. Light, not water, flooded into the passageway and I was staring at a burly, mustachioed man in a formal black dinner suit. His face was craggy and hard and he had a mouth that hung loose and ragged, like a torn pocket. Lewis Gorman was standing behind him.

"Boy, am I glad to see you," I said, stepping forward. "I was beginning to wonder if anybody was going to come along. I guess I got kind of lost—"

"Nobody in this house gets lost for very long, Mr. Billings. I told you the house has a brain. Every door in the house is hooked up to it, and an alarm is automatically set off when any of them is opened. This section of the house is off-limits to party guests."

"I'm really sorry. I was just using your bathroom and I got engrossed in your paintings and then I wandered into your office here. I guess I just got kind of carried away. I thought maybe I could take a look around before we did that interview, you know, to kind of get an idea of how—"

"I don't like snooping reporters, Mr. Billings. You will please take your friend and get out of my house immediately. I intend to call your editor tomorrow morning and give him a full report on your conduct tonight. Sam, show Mr. Billings out."

Sam and I went to the bar where we picked up Mike, who wanted to know what was wrong and why we had to leave so early and who Sam was and where Gorman was. Sam, whoever he was, turned out to be very helpful. He took the parking ticket and gave it to the attendant and waited for Mike's blue Merc to be brought up before returning inside.

Mike was already in the car and I was about to get in myself when an olive-green Ford convertible pulled up. The valet opened the car door and a woman stepped out. I put my hand over my face, but it was too late. She was staring at me when I got into the car.

"Get the hell out of here," I said.

Halfway down the hill, Mike asked, "What was that all about? Who was that girl?"

"Her name's Sascha. She says she's a witch. She knew Sheila Warren."

"She must also know Gorman."

"It looks that way. But she also knows me. And now Gorman knows I'm not Jacob Billings of the *Chronicle*."

"You think it means trouble?"

"I don't know. Gorman already had his doubts that my snooping wasn't just innocent blundering. Now he's sure."

"What do you think he'll do?"

"I wish I knew."

"What happened in there? You got caught, I take it."

"Smart boy. That whole house is honeycombed with passageways. I wandered down one of them and wound up downstairs, in a kind of storeroom. And in that storeroom Gorman keeps some pretty weird shit."

"Like what, for instance?"

"Whips and dildos and sets of handcuffs. I've heard Gorman is a queen, but it looks like he goes in for bondage in a big way, too."

"And he caught you inspecting all this stuff?"

"No. He caught me upstairs. I had to pick the locks on two doors to get into the storeroom, but I didn't notice that the first one was only pickable one-way."

"Then he doesn't know for sure what you saw."

"He knows. Every room in the house is hooked up with a silent alarm. That's why he came running. That boy Sam must be the house watchdog and he must have run to fetch Gorman when the alarm went off."

"What did Gorman say?"

"He looked a little pissed. He told me he was going to report me to my editor in the morning. Then he told me to get you and get out."

"Great. If he calls the paper, I'm screwed. Scratch one job."

"Sorry, Mike, I didn't mean to blow it for you. But I wouldn't start looking for another job yet. If Gorman is into

177

something really heavy, he might not want to stir things up. He'll just clam up about the whole thing."

"Even if he does call, I could probably save my job if I knew exactly why we were up there tonight."

"Sorry. No can do. I told you I'd let you know the whole thing when I found it out. I don't know it yet."

He didn't say anything more until we hit the beginning of the freeway. "You want to stop someplace and get a cup of coffee?"

"No, thanks. I've got some thinking to do. Take me home, will you?"

The rest of the trip was spent in silence. At least in the car it was silent. In my head, different possible combinations screamed and chattered and babbled and dissolved and recombined until I found myself on Bufort Street.

CHAPTER 18

The next day, I called Ellman and filled him in on developments, then phoned Mike to see if Gorman had called the paper. He hadn't. I lounged around the house until 6:30, then got up and got dressed. I put on an old pair of jeans and a dark sweater and a pair of tennies, grabbed my binoculars, and went down to the car.

I figured I'd get up to Malibu early so I could pick out a good stakeout position while it was still light. The sun was setting as I turned on Summit View Road, a huge, flattened-out, fiery ball sinking into the line of gray-brown haze that has come to infect even the seashore horizons of Los Angeles. I went slowly, surveying the sides of the road for a good place, but didn't see any. On the right, steep dirt cliffs ran straight up from the road and on the left, there was no vegetation anywhere that would provide any sort of a cover. I ran the car up on the sandy embankment at the end of the road, turned around and started back down.

The only place I could see where there was the slightest possibility of posting myself without being seen was at the southern tip of the flagstone wall. There was a mound of iceplant there and even though it wasn't near the gates of the property, I guessed it would have to do. At least I could watch the road and see who was coming and going.

I coasted down the hill toward the beach, thinking I'd get something to eat before starting my all-night vigil. The sun had already sunk below the horizon, leaving the brown blanket of smog streaked with yellow. The air was being

179

marked by the purposeful turnings of sea birds making their last plunges into the surf before darkness fell, making fishing impossible. The strip of lights that was Malibu was beginning to come alive—soft lights from houses, harsh neon reds and blues and oranges from restaurants and drive-ins and liquor stores and bars.

` At the foot of the hill, I turned north and drove about half a mile before finding a coffee shop that was open. I ordered some welsh rarebit and a pot of coffee and settled down in a booth by the window with a newspaper and waited for night.

At about eight-thirty, I paid my check to the gum-chewing waitress, who didn't seem too happy I had sat in her station killing space for over an hour. Her face loosened up when I gave her a dollar tip and she smiled and shoved the buck into the pocket of her uniform.

I parked the car within sight of my hiding place, took out the binocs and locked the car. I trudged up to my little mound of iceplant and lay down behind it. A steady, wet evening breeze blew in from the ocean, and pierced my sweater. Soon I was cold.

An hour passed and no cars came up the hill. Two hours. Dead silence, except for the faint stirrings of the wind. A siren screamed its lament somewhere far below on the thickly inhabited stretch of fun-sand highway.

Three hours and just Jake Asch and the breeze. I thought I should have brought a deck of cards, but discarded the idea immediately, realizing how hard it would be to play solitaire in the dark on iceplant. But then, on a stakeout, you can get all kinds of strange ideas. After three or four hours of sitting, doing nothing, just waiting for something to happen, you can start to go a little crackers. Things like the little red lights blinking on and off on the wings of an airplane start to excite you. You begin to play mind games with yourself, making up some exotic destination and story to tag to the plane and its cargo. I watched one through the binoculars for nearly twenty minutes as it made its way across the black indifferent night sky. It was carrying a cache of automatic rifles to the guerrillas in Guatemala. I wished I were on it.

About midnight, the moon came out to keep me company. I sneaked around the wall by the cliff that fell down to the sea, and took a look at the house through the binoculars. Everything was dark and still. I went back to my position and watched the road.

At 3:31, headlights came around the corner and up the hill, temporarily blinding me. They stopped by my car and a spotlight shone through the window. Private Security Patrol. I saw the rent-a-cop silhouetted in the beams of his headlights as he moved around in front of his car and put his flash to the windows of mine, looking for registration. He tried the doors, looked around, then got back in his car, presumably figuring that anybody who was planning to burglarize a house would want a fast getaway and wouldn't lock his car. Pretty sound theorizing, especially for a rent-a-cop.

The patrol car came up the hill, and the security cop sprayed his spot along the sides of the road. I slid back from the edge of the mound of iceplant and lay as flat as possible to let the spotlight swing over me. At the top of the hill, he turned around and went back down.

I looked at the luminous dial of my watch, pulled out my pad and took note of the time. I did it because there was nothing else to do and I don't like going home with an empty pad. After all, you've got to have something to show for seven hours' work.

At four, I decided I'd had enough. I was tired and hungry

and cold and badly in need of a hot shower. I somehow made it home through the soft blur of freeway lights, took a shower, and collapsed into the softness of my bed. I didn't get up until one the next afternoon.

CHAPTER 19

Although I was better prepared physically and psychologically for the wetness of the ocean night, the second evening passed about the same as the first—cold and boring.

On the third night I decided there was absolutely no sense in going up to Gorman's house again, that there would probably be nothing to see and it was senseless to spend another miserable night shivering behind a mound of iceplant. So I got in my car and drove out to Malibu.

At 12:32 I got an inkling that my luck had started to change. Lights struck the side of the wall and a dark, late-model convertible drove up the hill. I couldn't get the license number, but I recognized the car. It was Sascha's. A good ten minutes elapsed between the first and second cars. It was a light-colored Continental and this time I was better with the plates—CJC 441. When three more cars followed shortly thereafter, I thought Gorman must be having another party, then looked at the time and thought better of it.

It was almost ten past one when the blue Ford van made its way slowly up the hill, its engine roaring in protest of the weight it was being forced to pull. I took down the plate number and watched it pull up to the front gates and flash its lights and disappear.

I knew it would be risky trying to sneak a glimpse of whatever was going on up at the house. There might be other cars coming and once caught out in the open, my cover would be blown. I sat there arguing with myself back and forth and after a few more minutes passed and no more cars seemed to be arriving, I decided to go up and take the chance. I ran up the steep hill to the iron gates and stopped at the edge of the driveway to catch my breath.

Ducking under the eye of the closed-circuit camera, I poked my head around the gate post. The van was sitting in the driveway by the front door, its back doors standing wide open. The inside was empty.

The front door of the house opened then and two men stepped into the rectangle of light that shone onto the flagstone walk. I couldn't make out the faces, since their backs were to the light, but then one of them turned around to say goodnight and I caught the profile. There was no mistaking that nose. The other man on the doorstep waved a goodnight and went back into the house. Eberhardt went around to the back of the van, closed and locked the doors, and walked around to the front and slid behind the steering wheel.

I ducked under the television camera once again and started to run back along the wall. I'd made about twenty yards when I slipped on a patch of wet grass and fell, my foot turning and the pain shooting up my leg as something went in my ankle, and I went down. I took the fall on my shoulder, rolled, sprang back up, and kept on running. I looked back and saw the gates open, and tried to run faster, but every time I put my foot down, the pain ran clear up into my thigh. I looked back again and saw the headlights of the van coming through the gates and said to hell with it and opened up into a sprint. I dove into the iceplant and the van pulled by me, heading down toward the beachfront. I didn't think he saw me.

It was three-twenty by the time all the cars had come back down from Gorman's place, and by that time, the swelling of my ankle had increased proportionately with the pain. I loosened the laces of my shoe and let the cold seep in and numb my foot. I limped to the car, tossed the binoculars into the front seat and started down the hill. I had just turned onto the Pacific Coast Highway when Eberhardt passed me in the van going the opposite way.

I swung around, went half a block past Summit View, and parked in the parking lot of a real estate office. Ten minutes later, the van hit the bottom of the hill and headed south down the highway. There were only a handful of other cars on the road and it was easy to keep a safe distance between us without losing sight of him.

He went through the tunnel onto the Santa Monica Freeway and went all the way down to Western before getting off. He went north on Western to Wilshire, hung a right and drove a few blocks and pulled into the driveway of Brown Brothers Funeral Home.

I passed the driveway, went up two blocks and turned up a side street and parked. I opened the trunk and got a chisel and a screwdriver out of my toolbox, dropped them in my pocket, and walked down to Wilshire. Except for a few straggling motorists, the street was deserted. I walked down to Brown Brothers and turned down the gap that ran between the building and the used electrical supplies store next door, and looked for a window. I found one and tried it. Locked. I spotted another one a few yards down, but it wouldn't budge, either, so I worked the screwdriver underneath the sash, forcing it upward until I could get the chisel in. I leaned on the chisel and the lock broke open with a bang. I dropped down below the window and waited for the sound of footsteps. Nothing. After a few minutes, I straightened up and slid the window open and hoisted myself in.

The curtains on the other side of the window were thick and dark and smelled of dust. The lights were off in the room, so I drew the curtains a little so I could see.

I was in the chapel. Directly in front of me a bier stood

185

empty between two tall metal candelabras, and beyond the bier and facing it were rows of metal folding chairs. Over to one side there was a small alcove lined with curtains and filled with more folding chairs. Next to it was a door.

I went to the door and cracked it open. The hallway was very dimly lighted and empty. I stepped out into it and listened. I could hear muffled voices, and I began to make my way slowly toward them. They were coming from a pair of closed doors at the end of the hallway. On the wall beside the doors, a tiny red light shone brightly, warning me that the room was in use.

When I listened at the doors, all I could hear was one voice. It was Eberhardt. At first I thought he might be talking to one of the stiffs he drove around all day, but then I heard another voice, soft, almost whispering, and I knew that whoever was in there with him was alive. Eberhardt's voice grew suddenly louder.

"I'm telling you, goddamn it, I want more money. You two got this whole thing worked out and I'm just the god-damn delivery boy. Well that's okay, but this delivery boy can throw a monkey wrench into your nice little setup and don't think he won't."

"Calm down, for god's sake. There's nothing to get all worked up about. We'll talk about it later."

"Later, hell. We'll talk about it now. I want more money. Otherwise I go to the cops."

"All right, all right. Go into the office and we'll work it out. I've got some things to take care of in here and I'll be in in a minute."

I knew I didn't have time to make it down to the chapel, so I tried the first door handle I found and ducked inside, just as the other door opened. I closed the door as gently as I could, leaving it open a crack so that it wouldn't make any noise closing. The room was pitch-black and I couldn't see my hand in front of my face. I could hear footsteps

186

moving down the hall toward me and I stepped back from the door. My foot hit something and I lost my balance. I reached a hand out to brace myself and it came down on something hard and heavy and I felt it move and heard something fall over. I stood upright and felt for the wall, found it, and spread out against it behind the door and held my breath. The footsteps had stopped. Then I heard them again, just outside the door.

The door swung open slowly and the light from the hallway fell into the room, across the display of empty caskets. I leaned over, cocked my fist back and shifted all my weight to my right side, and waited for the shadow in the box of light on the floor to move. It moved. The man stepped into the room and I swung, putting everything I had into it. The punch caught him flush on the face and I felt his nose splinter. He hit the door and slammed it shut and I couldn't see anymore. I lunged at the door and gathered two handfuls of coat from the darkness. A hand scratched my face and I heard him grunting and caught a gust of rank breath as I hit him hard in the stomach, then twice more in the head. There was a shooting pain in my hand as I hit something harder than his head—maybe the floor—and then light splashed on us from the hallway and the lights in the room went on.

"That's enough," a voice said behind me.

I looked up and blinked and then I froze. The hole made by a .357 could play hell with one's digestive tract. Mr. Peeples was looking at me with a steady gaze. The hand holding the gun was steady, too.

"Get up."

I got up. Eberhardt did too, but his legs were shaky. He leaned back against the wall, holding his stomach and sucking in lungfuls of air, or at least trying to. His nose, that monumental piece of engineering, was wider now and flat, and was pouring blood all over his mouth and chin. "He broke my fucking nose, the son of a bitch," he managed to say between gasps.

"Shut up and search him."

Eberhardt wiped some of the blood on the sleeve of his coat and moved forward. He came up with the screwdriver and chisel. "The son of a bitch broke my nose," he said again, almost whimpering, He took a handkerchief out of his pocket and tried to plug up the bleeding.

"Turn around," Peeples said.

He wasn't smiling, but there didn't seem to be any malice in his voice. I didn't like it, but there wasn't much I could do about it, so I turned around. I didn't hear it coming, but that's not particularly unusual. There was a lot of pain and a lot of light flooding into my head all at once—too much to think about, so my brain decided to go to sleep for a while.

Paul Ellman came to me then. He was wearing glasses with green shade lenses fastened to them and a Pancho Villa mustache and he was trying to sell me a Monte Carlo Duraseal metal casket with a Fog-Mist finish and 600 Cheney Velvet interior. I told him I'd think about it, and commented on how nice the Egyptian symbols looked drawn in blood on his forehead.

CHAPTER 20

When I opened my eyes, the sun exploded into them and I closed them quickly again. I was on my back and the sun was directly overhead, so I figured it had to be noon. I licked my lips. They were dry. Noon. Jesus.

I tried to move my hands up to my aching head, but nothing happened. I couldn't feel them at all. It took me a few long seconds to determine that I couldn't feel them because I was lying on top of them and the weight of my body had numbed them into insensibility. I tried bringing them out from underneath me, but they wouldn't come. Then I felt the ropes.

I turned my head away from the sun and cracked my eyes slowly, blinking back the pain and dizziness. I looked around. I was on a table. A long, white, cool table. When I looked at it obliquely, I could see that the sun was attached to the ceiling. I was in a room. Three pats on the back for the ace private detective.

The room had the scrubbed and disinfected look of surgery. The walls were white tile and against one of them two glass cabinets stood filled with bottles of various sizes and colors. A few yards away from me, some surgical instruments were laid out on a movable white tray and beside it rested a large, odd-looking machine. The machine was glass and metal and from its middle sprouted two rubber hoses, each of which tapered down to a long, ominous-looking needle. Just beyond the machine was another long table like the one I was on. A sheet was covering something

189

on the table and the something had a generally human shape. The shape wasn't moving. Aside from the something under the sheet, I was alone in the room.

I tried to move my right foot, and when both of them moved, I looked down to see what was the matter. My feet were being held together by some sort of wooden device roughly resembling stocks, which was fastened over my ankles. I rolled over onto one shoulder to relieve some of the pressure on my hands and tried to work them loose from the ropes, but whoever had tied them had known what he was doing, and I gave up after a few minutes. I rolled off the table and landed on my back, trying to keep my feet up to prevent the stocks from hitting the floor. I struggled to my knees, then onto my feet, and hopped toward the surgical instruments on the tray.

There was a scalpel, an auger, two pairs of forceps, a pair of scissors, clamps, and some jars of cosmetics. The scalpel looked promising, but it also looked sharp, and considering the condition of my hands, I decided to try the scissors first. I turned around and felt around on the tray behind me until my fingers found the scissors. Then the door in front of me opened and Eberhardt stepped into the room. His nose was still a mess and his eyes were almost swollen shut, but he was smiling. He closed the door behind him.

"So, Sleeping Beauty's up and around already. What're you doing over there? Being a bad boy, I bet."

I tried to figure some way to turn around and stab him with the scissors, but I couldn't come up with any. He walked over to me. His nose looked even more messy up close.

"What you got there behind your back?"

I didn't answer him. I didn't figure it was going to make much difference to his attitude one way or another. He hit me in the solar plexus and I doubled over, sucking for air, and the scissors clattered to the floor.

"I knew you were being a bad boy."

He caught me under the armpits and dragged me back to the table and sat me on it. Then he lifted my feet back onto it and I was staring into the sun again. His face leered over me.

"See this?" He was pointing to his nose. "You broke it, you son of a bitch."

My chest was rattling, trying to locate some air somewhere, and it took me everything I had to say it. "You should thank me. It would've cost you $500 to get that thing fixed anywhere else."

"A joker, huh? Well, here, joker, see what kind of a joke you can make out of this—"

He was slow. I saw it coming and moved my head to one side and his fist glanced off my cheek. I wasn't so lucky with the next one. It caught me flush on the mouth and drove my head back into the table. I tasted blood. He raised his fist again and I moved to the right and he missed completely. I heard something crack on the hard table. He howled with pain and grabbed his hand. He hopped around on one foot for a few seconds, holding his hand and swearing. Then suddenly he wheeled around, took a quick step down the table, and hit me in the balls, hard. My body convulsed and the pain instantly filled my intestines, then my stomach. I vomited and passed out.

When I woke up, Eberhardt was leering over me again. "You like that one, do you, Sleeping Beauty?"

I wanted to spit in his face, but the nausea had possession of my body, and I didn't have the strength. He moved away somewhere and when he came back, he was holding one of the hoses with the long, shiny needle on it. "Know what this is? You're a smart guy. I thought for sure you'd know. It's called a trocar. It's used in embalming. The needle here is hollow, see, and it's attached to that machine there, which is a pump. What you do, see, is stick this needle in the

191

stomach and it just pumps out everything in the chest cavity and intestinal tract. Just sucks it all right out. You want to see how it works?"

Adrenalin shot into my bloodstream, temporarily dampening the waves of nausea that welled up from my intestines, and I watched the needle as he poised it above my stomach like a picador about to stick a bull. A voice sounded from behind him.

"Put that down. It's not a toy."

Eberhardt turned around.

Peeples walked over to the table and took the needle out of Eberhardt's hand. He looked down at me, then back at him, angrily. "I told you to watch him, not mutilate him."

"He broke my nose."

Peeples looked disgusted. "Get out of here."

"You don't talk to me that way. I told you things are going to be different from now on. I'm not your fucking errand boy."

"Yes, you told me. Now get out of here. Go to the office and stay there until I get there."

Eberhardt looked at him sideways, muttered something, then went out the door, past two men I hadn't noticed before. One of them was Gorman's bodyguard, Sam.

Peeples pulled me up by the shoulders into a sitting position and swung my feet over the edge of the table.

"Thanks."

He didn't say I was welcome. He bent down and unfastened the stocks from my ankles.

"What is that thing anyway?"

"It's called a Throop Foot Positioner. It's used in caskets to hold bent or deformed legs in a straight position."

"Charming. How long have I been out?"

"You've been here about half an hour."

That took me by surprise. It seemed more like two days.

I stood up. My legs were shaking violently, but they held me.

"Can you walk?"

"I don't know. I think so."

I took a couple of steps. "How about untying my hands?"

Peeples looked at Sam, who nodded, and Peeples turned me around and I felt a tingling sensation in my hands. Then Peeples led me over to where Sam and the other man were standing. When I got close, they both made faces and reared back.

"Jesus Christ, he's puked on himself. He stinks."

"I can't very well help that. It's Ronald's fault. I told him to watch him and make sure he doesn't get away and this is what happened. I told Mr. Gorman there was going to be trouble, that Ronald was getting out of hand and that I—"

"Yeah, yeah, okay. We'll take care of it later. Right now my orders are to take this guy up to Mr. Gorman and I can't take him like this. He stinks. You got a fresh suit of clothes in this joint?"

"Yes, I think I've got something that will fit him. I'll go see."

"Is there a shower around here somewhere?"

"Uh, down the hall, third door on the right."

Sam turned to me. "Let's go." He reached in his pocket and pulled out a large black sap and tapped it a couple of times in his hand. "And don't get any smart ideas. Otherwise your brains might get loosened more than they already are."

We walked down the hall. Sam went into the bathroom first to check things out, then motioned me in. "Get out of those clothes and wash real good."

"Certainly. I wouldn't want to smell bad for Mr. Gorman." He stationed his buddy in the doorway and left the

193

door open, and he stayed inside and watched me get undressed.

After a couple of minutes in the shower, Sam told me that was enough, and as I stepped out of the glass door, he threw a towel in my face.

"Your new clothes are here," he said, pointing to a pile of clothing on the toilet seat. "Let's get a move on."

The suit was dark and a little conservative for my taste, but it fit all right. As soon as I got the jacket on, Sam grabbed my arm. "Okay, let's go."

"Just a minute," I said, and wrenched my arm free. I went over and fished around in my soiled suit for my wallet and car keys. My money was missing out of the wallet.

"That baboon took my money."

"We'll lodge a formal complaint with the management. Come on."

He led me down the hall and out the back door to a black Mercedes limousine that was parked in the rear courtyard. He pushed me into the back seat and slid in next to me and the other one, whose name I gathered was Reed, drove.

By the time we got onto the Santa Monica Freeway, my head was throbbing where Peeples had laid the gun across my skull. I put my head back on the seat and closed my eyes, trying to shut out the pain, then wondered what closing your eyes had to do with pain, and opened them again. "What are we—"

"Shut up."

"Hey, but lis—"

"Just shut up."

I shut up. The lights were off in the house when we pulled up to the gates, and the driveway was deserted, except for a dark-colored Ford convertible.

"Childe Harold to the dark tower came."

Either my traveling companions didn't hear the remark or they didn't care to comment on my choice of quotes.

194

Probably the latter. The gates opened for us and we pulled up in front of the door. Reed got out and held the car door open while Sam and I got out.

There was a fire going in the Swedish fireplace when we came in, and Sascha was sprawled across one of the couches, enjoying it. She looked up and smiled.

"You don't look so good, Mr. Private Pig."

"I can't say the same for you, my dear. You look simply ravishing tonight."

I felt Sam's fingers in my back telling me that it was time to move. We went through the hallway, turned under the archway, went down the steps and stopped in front of the metal door I'd tried the night of the party. Sam reached over my shoulder and pressed a button by the door. A buzzer sounded and the lock released its grip. Sam told Reed to stay outside and we went through the door into a narrow passageway, the walls of which were covered with thick cloth padding. There was another metal door at the end of the passageway. It buzzed open as we approached.

The room we entered was dark. It was a small theater which would, when full, have seated about fifty people. The seats were divided into two equal sections; a small aisle ran between them. Gorman was sitting in an aisle seat, his back to us, watching the movie that was running on the screen down front. There were two figures on the screen, a gagged and bound nude boy who looked to be in his early teens and an older man who was wearing a beard and a bathrobe and a malicious grin that said many things, none of them nice. Next to the movie screen was a panel of closed-circuit television screens similar to the panel I had seen in the office across the hall. Reed was cleaning his fingernails on one of the screens; Sascha was lying by the livingroom fireplace on another; the padded passageway just outside the door was another; the rest showed different parts of the house and grounds.

"What took you so long?"

"We ran into some trouble. Peeples's driver had worked him over and we had to get him in walking condition."

Gorman pressed a button on the arm of his chair and the lights in the room came on and the black and white celluloid image on the screen flickered and died, postponing the fate of the bound boy.

He stood up and faced us. He was wearing a blue and yellow paisley smoking jacket, blue navy slacks and a pair of yellow cloth bedroom slippers. "I'll want to talk to you about that later. Something will obviously have to be done. You may wait outside. Stay close in case I need you."

Sam went out and closed the door and I watched him take his place on the panel of screens, in between Reed and Sascha.

"Efficient boy."

"For what I pay him, I expect him to be. Have a seat, Mr. Asch."

"Thanks, but I think I'll stand."

"As you wish. Would you care for a drink? A brandy, perhaps? You look as if you could use it."

"No thanks."

"I'm sorry about your getting hurt tonight."

"That's the breaks. Part of the trade."

"Yes, I suppose so. Still I can assure you that I had never intended that you get hurt. I abhor violence and only condone it when it is absolutely necessary."

"Look, Gorman, you didn't have me brought up here to apologize for Eberhardt's beating me up. What do you want?"

"My, my, you are an impatient man, aren't you? Relax. Everything will be explained in good time, I promise you."

"I've been hit on the head and maybe got a concussion. I've been beaten up and nearly ruptured. I've lost a good suit of clothes and had some baboon steal all the money out of my wallet. I'm afraid I'm beyond the relaxing stage."

"You're quite sure you wouldn't care for a brandy?"

"Yes, I'm quite sure. I just want to know what you want with me so I can go home and get some sleep."

He leaned back on one of the seats, bracing himself with his two perfectly manicured hands. The movement was made as all his movements were, slowly and deliberately, as if part of some sacred dance. "I've had you brought here for one purpose and one purpose only—to reason with you. You are a reasonable man, aren't you, Mr. Asch?"

"Why bother with reason? Why not just have Sam there sap me to death and dump the body in Malibu Canyon. It'd probably save you a lot of time and me a lot of headaches."

He looked surprised. "Is there some reason I should want you dead?"

"I don't know, is there?"

"Apparently you think there is. You think that I'm responsible for the deaths of Sheila Warren and Randy Folsom and Christopher Ruane. And you think that since I know you know that I should want you dead. But you see, your original supposition is erroneous and therefore everything that follows is also erroneous. I'm not responsible for anyone's death. The killing of Sheila Warren was the result of a disastrous miscalculation in judgment, nothing more. And poor Christopher was killed by his own greed."

"Don't tell me you had me brought up here in the middle of the night to convince me you had nothing to do with those murders."

"I didn't say I had nothing to do with them, just that I was not responsible for them."

"And you had me brought up here to explain the subtle difference."

"No, I had you brought up here because you stuck your nose where it didn't belong and got caught. But actually, that doesn't make me too terribly unhappy. Believe it or

197

not, Mr. Asch, I came to the conclusion sometime ago that this meeting was going to be necessary. After Sascha told me you'd been in Isis asking all sorts of questions, I did some research on you. You have a reputation for being a very tenacious man, did you know that?"

He paused for a second, but the question sounded rhetorical so I didn't answer it. He went on.

"I thought at first I could discourage your inquisitiveness by applying a little gentle pressure, but after you failed to respond, I realized you would continue to dig until you came up with the truth. But the truth, you see, is subject to misinterpretation, and I would rather show it to you on my own ground, where I still exert some measure of control, than have you stumble on it when and where I can't find you."

"So you're the one who gave my credit rating a nose-bleed. The mysterious Mr. Jones."

"Yes."

"Then you knew who I was at the party."

"That took me by surprise. I knew you would eventually wind up here, but I never expected it would be so soon. All I had seen of you was your photograph. Seeing you in the flesh was a bit of a shock."

"You never let on you knew."

"Of course not. It would have tipped my hand. But it was then I decided that I could use a man of your talents, that it would be perhaps to our mutual advantage to team up."

"Team up how?"

"I am willing to pay you fifty thousand dollars to find the killer of Christopher Ruane."

"Why?"

"Because whoever killed Christopher has something that could be quite troublesome for me, and I want it back."

"Like a film, for instance?"

"You are very astute."

198

"Why don't you send one of your boys to find the film? Why me?"

"Because I want to put as much distance as I can between myself and Christopher's murder, not get closer to it. If anybody in my employ began asking a lot of questions, it might stir up a lot of inquisitiveness I would rather be spared. Besides, you've already done considerable work on those films. You've been closer to the situation than anybody except the police. Therefore you're the most likely man for the job."

I stared at him and he stared back. Nothing was exchanged in the transaction. "Ruane killed Sheila Warren, didn't he?"

"Yes."

"Under your orders?"

"No, no. Of course not."

"Ruane was working for you."

"That's correct. You see now what I mean about the facts being subject to misinterpretation? You can see why I felt this little session to be necessary. Let me explain the entire situation—"

"Please do."

"I first met Randy Folsom eight years ago. I was interested in his work at that time—it embodied a fire then that later went out. We struck up a relationship—one that later became rather burdensome for me. Randy had a penchant for getting into trouble—financial and otherwise—and he always came running to me to get him out. It got to be too much to bear and I finally told him not to come around here anymore. That was three years ago. Then one day about five months ago, he turned up here with Sheila. Sheila was a member of a little group that used to meet up here occasionally. She had met Randy a few months previously and he had moved in with her, as you know. She suggested to me that we have Randy film one of our group's meetings,

199

and I agreed, after much soul-searching. I arranged to buy the negative and a print for one thousand dollars. I found out only later that Randy had made extra prints and kept them."

"Did he try to put the bite on you?"

"No, but he probably would have gotten around to it. The situation was clearly out of hand. You cannot allow children to have access to dangerous toys, or somebody is bound to get hurt. Unfortunately, the toys fell out of the hands of one child and into those of another."

"Ruane."

"Yes. I sent Christopher to get the films back and to discourage Randy from launching into any other similar business ventures. Christopher could be quite persuasive when he had to be. When he came back that night, he was in a highly nervous condition. He told me that Randy had gotten belligerent and had threatened to turn the films over to the press. He said that a fight ensued and he'd been forced to kill Randy in self-defense. He had killed Sheila because she had been a witness. As I was involved by circumstance, I had to cover up for him. I was grieved over Sheila's death, but as you can see there was little else I could do."

"And you didn't think there was anything phony about his story?"

"No, I didn't. I must confess I was completely taken in. You see, Christopher brought me back the films. He told me he had had to torture Sheila to find out where they were, but he brought them back to me. What I didn't know at the time was that Randy had made two extra prints of the films he had made and that Christopher had kept the extras, intending to pick up where Folsom had left off."

"It doesn't make any sense. How far did he think he was going to get with blackmail? He had to know you'd find out about it once he started to send the word out that he had the films and put a stop to it."

He picked up one of his slippered feet, turned it over in the air and looked at it. "Christopher had become mentally unstable, Mr. Asch. His greed prevented him from seeing that far into the future. I first got an inkling of it when he was living at this house. I found out he was selling drugs, so I immediately ordered him to move out. The salary I was paying him was more than generous, but his avarice knew no bounds. The fact that he was jeopardizing my entire social position by his activities held no importance for him. Christopher was the disastrous result of a "My Fair Lady" experiment. It just proves the adage, you can't make a silk purse out of a sow's ear."

"But you still kept him on your payroll after that."

"For precisely that reason. He'd become untrustworthy and I felt it desirable to keep an eye on him. That was the cheapest way I could think of to do it and to make sure he would keep his mouth shut."

"Also maybe because he was your lover?"

I thought maybe that would get a rise out of him, but his face remained impassive, drained of color and emotion. "That part of our relationship ended long ago. It was replaced by a purely business relationship."

"What kind of business relationship?"

"You might say Christopher was a procurer. I sent him out to get me things. All sorts of things."

I somehow didn't think he meant hot pastrami sandwiches. "And he was the one who made the contact with Eberhardt and made the payoffs."

He squeezed a slender fist in the air as if he had hold of some small, helpless animal and was pressing the air out of its body. Then he opened the hand and peered into the palm. I wondered if he saw me there, squashed and lifeless.

"Let me give you a piece of sound advice, Mr. Asch. I've let you poke around at will up to this time, simply because it was to my advantage to do so. But don't let your inquisitive nature get out of bounds. Asking too many questions could have the effect of diminishing your popularity."

"I'll try to remember that."

"Please do."

"To tell me all you've told me—assuming I believe it all —you must be pretty confident I'll accept your offer."

"I am."

"Why?"

"Simply because you are a reasonable man, as I said before, a man who is capable of seeing alternatives clearly and acting logically on those alternatives."

"And what are my alternatives?"

"You have none." His voice softened and he sounded like a patient teacher explaining an elementary algebra problem to a rather dimwitted child. "I have closed off any alternatives you might have had by closing off my own. By telling you what I've told you tonight, I've purposely committed myself to a position from which I can't back down —like a soldier who shoots his horse to prevent himself from retreating. Do you understand what I'm saying?"

"You're saying that although killing me might prove to be a great inconvenience that if I didn't accept your offer, you'd have to do it."

He looked pleased that the day's lesson had sunk in. "Precisely."

"I've got a question."

"Yes?"

"How are you so sure that Ruane was killed for the films?"

"Because the films were nowhere to be found after Christopher was found dead. And because Christopher had an accomplice helping him when he went up to the Warren house. Find the accomplice and you find who has the films."

"How do you know all this?"

"It's not important how I know. I know, that's all."

"Well, say I find the murderer and he doesn't particularly feel like giving me the films. Then what?"

"I don't want you to get the films back. All I want you to do is find out who killed Christopher. When you do that and report back to me, your job is finished."

"And that's all?"

"That's all."

"And then I get the fifty G's?"

"The money will be paid in $10,000 installments which will be deposited in your bank account at the first of every year."

"Wait a minute. That means I won't get the whole amount for five years."

His small eyes glistened. "I have to take some precautions. You wouldn't expect me to leave myself completely unprotected. What if you decided to take the money and then tell somebody what you know? In five years, the Warren murders will be history."

"And in five years, I couldn't talk and not get prosecuted for concealing evidence."

"As I say, I have to take some precautions."

I could feel the bite of the traps he was laying for me. I saw myself in five years, procuring things for Gorman, struggling uselessly against the ropes he had tied me with, like that bound boy on the screen. He must have seen it, too, because he smiled.

"Okay. But I want the first ten thousand in advance."

"When you find Christopher's murderer."

"I'll need expense money."

"I will give you one thousand dollars. That should more than cover any expenses you might incur."

"Okay then."

"Good. You see, I knew you were my type of man from the beginning."

"What kind of man is that?"

"A man who can see his alternatives clearly and act quickly and decisively on those alternatives. I'll get you a check and then we can have a drink on our newly formed relationship."

He went over to the control panel. "Sam, go into my office and get a blank check and bring it in here, please."

Gorman turned his back to me and started to say something, but he never got it out. I came up behind him and slipped an arm around his neck. He tried to yell, but the chokehold was tight and the only thing that came out was a muffled gurgling noise. He thrashed around and his hand jerked back, trying to claw my face, and I watched the fingers flex and unflex with a strange fascination. The hand shriveled into a stiff claw and then suddenly went limp, and I let him down easy to the ground.

I had to work fast. I pulled the sash out of his robe and tied his hands as tightly as I could behind his back with it. Then I ripped a piece from his sleeve and stuffed it into his mouth, keeping one eye on the television screen that showed the padded hallway. I reached underneath his arms and dragged him back between two rows of seats so that he couldn't be seen from the door. I looked around the room and spotted some metal folding chairs stacked against the far wall, selected a nice, heavy one and went back behind the door to wait for Sam. My hands started sweating and I began to plan out mentally how I was going to hit him when he came in. I didn't feel like getting that sap across the side of my head.

Sam was on the screen now. He was talking to Reed and he had a check in his hand. A buzzer rang next to me. There were two buttons in front of me on the wall. I pressed the one marked OUTER DOOR, and Sam was on another screen, walking down the padded hallway. I pressed the button marked INNER DOOR, stood back and brought the chair back to get a good swing.

The door opened and Sam walked in. I swung the chair. It caught him across the eyes and he went down. He started to get up, but I brought the chair down across his head and he settled back down. I bent down and went through his pockets. I came up with the sap, which I dropped into my own pocket. I started to move away, but heard a noise, and when I turned around, Sam was on his knees. Some guys never learn. I hit him with the sap behind the ear and he fell forward on his face and lay still. Then I went into the projection booth.

I found what I was looking for in a plain brown film can marked, "Ritual," on a shelf with about thirty other films. I unwound the film that was on the projector, threaded "Ritual" through the machine and turned it on.

The screen was completely dark at first and then an organ began to play an eerie dirge and I could see vague shapes emerging out of the darkness. Almost in rhythm with the organ music, there came a chanting, softly at first, then louder, in a strange language I couldn't identify. Then something stirred and a bluish light billowed out from the center of the screen, revealing a still and naked white form lying across a stone slab. The eyes of the naked man were open, but there was no life behind them. Rising darkly into the air, from the harness strapped to the corpse's thighs, was a huge black leather dildo.

At the head and feet of the corpse were the cobra candleholders in which black candles were sputtering. Around the stone slab, drawn on the floor in white, was a double white circle marked with the Egyptian symbols for the genii of death.

The circle of blue light spread and I could see that the

chanting was being done by four black-robed, candle-bearing figures who were standing in a semicircle around the corpse on the stone altar. The figures were wearing grotesque animal masks; one had the head of a hawk, another a wolf, another an ape, and on the shoulders of the one on the end sat the huge and distorted head of a bald man.

Above and behind the altar, two more figures, also dressed in black robes, watched the proceedings from an elevated platform. One, who was seated on a black throne, had the head of a jackal. I recognized him from my recent studies in Egyptology as Anubis, the Lord of the Cemetery. His arms were folded across his chest and in one hand he held a scepter and in the other, an ankh. The other figure, standing beside the throne, had the incredibly ugly, green head of a crocodile. On either side of the two was a tall iron brazier. I didn't know if it were an optical illusion or a very tricky ventilating system, but black smoke rose out of the braziers in two perfect columns, straight up toward the ceiling.

The chanting and the organ music suddenly stopped and the crocodile-head stepped forward and began reciting some litany in the same strange language, and below, the other four figures repeated the words responsively. The crocodile finished and stepped back. Then Anubis raised his scepter and one of the figures below removed its mask and glided toward the stone table. It was Sheila Warren. She bent and kissed the lips of the lifeless form on the altar slowly, passionately, then resumed her place with the others. Another figure came out of the group and pulled off its mask. It was Sascha. She went through the ritual kiss and refilled the gap in the semicircle. The other two were men, neither of whom I recognized and after they went through the procedure, all four turned toward the platform, where the high priestess had shed her crocodile head and black robes. She was naked and down on one knee, holding a

206

goblet out to the jackal on the throne, who took it from her and drank. She stood and turned slowly, the blue light swimming in the slim, smooth contours of her body and I saw the face. The face.

She started down the stairs with the chalice, murmuring a barely audible incantation, which was picked up by the other four. She stopped in front of the altar and poured the liquid from the cup over the body of the dead man, and while the others were stripping off their robes, she climbed up on the stone table and mounted the corpse.

I'd seen enough. I didn't want to get any sicker than I already felt. I rewound the film, put it back in its can, and went out with it.

Reed looked surprised when I opened the outer door and brought the sap down across his head. The keys to the Mercedes were in his pocket.

Sascha jumped off the couch when I walked into the living room, the film tucked underneath my arm.

"Catchya later, Sascha baby," I said as I hit the front door.

I started the Mercedes, put it in drive, made a U-turn across the lawn and punched out. The tires slipped on the wet grass, then got some traction, and the car took off. I ran down a lawn statue of a little curly headed boy peeing on the lawn and I must have been going thirty by the time I hit the gates. They smashed open, one of them flying completely off its hinges, and when I got down to the bottom of the hill, I got out to check the damage. The front of the car was bashed in pretty good, but both headlights were working. I figured Gorman could afford the repair bill.

I drove back down to where my car was parked around the corner from Brown Brothers, and left the Mercedes, after wiping it down for prints. I got into my own car and drove down to Sheriff's Homicide and dropped the film off with the desk sergeant with a note and told him to be sure to give them both to Al Herrera in the morning and to tell him I would get in touch with him tomorrow sometime and explain everything.

I figured I could swear out a warrant for Gorman for kidnaping later. This morning I didn't want to be bogged down with a lot of bureaucratic red tape. There were things to be done.

CHAPTER 21

The lights were all off in the house, but then I didn't expect them to be on at four in the morning. I leaned on the doorbell until I heard a "Coming, coming" from somewhere deep inside. The tiny peephole door opened and an eye peered out.

There was a fumbling of locks and she was standing there in a bathrobe, trying to brush back a wave of long, bed-tousled hair that had fallen across her eyes.

"For God's sake, darling, what time is it?"

"I told you I'd be over when I cracked the case. Consider it cracked."

She just stood in the doorway staring at me.

"Offer me a drink and I'll tell you all about it."

She hesitated, then drew back the door and stepped aside. I walked into the living room and went over to the liquor tray and made myself a bourbon and water.

"Like one?"

"All right."

I made her a scotch and handed it to her and we both sat down. The liquor was deliciously warm going down, filling my chest with a false sense of well-being. We sat for a while, not saying anything, just sipping the drinks.

"So tell me about the case. How did it come out?"

"You know, Gloria, no matter how long you live, how much you see, you can never see it all. You know what I mean? Take tonight, for instance. Now, I've been around. No world traveler, you understand, but I've been a few places. Seen things that would turn an ordinary man's stomach. But just when you get to thinking you've seen it all, you find out you haven't seen anything."

"What did you see tonight that was so unusual?"

"A picture. A movie. Sort of a documentary."

"What was it about?"

"Necrophilia."

"Necrophilia?"

"Yeah, necrophilia. Get out your Krafft-Ebing. Necrophilia—the sexual lust for dead bodies."

"Sounds charming."

"Yeah, it was. See, it was all about this very rich and powerful pervert who lived in a big house on a hill. And through the years, this man had come to be possessed by an overpowering obsession to control everything he could touch. People, things, everything. And this obsession for control also spread over into his sex life, see, and he found he could only get stimulated by a sexual object he could completely dominate. First, he got his jollies off by tying people up, but when that started getting old, he started looking around for something else.

"Well, he found this friendly mortician whose business had fallen off and who was hard up for cash, and the two of them worked out an arrangement whereby the rich man would pay to rent a corpse for an evening. Just picture the scene of an unmarked black van pulling up to the huge house on the hill late at night, depositing its load, and then sliding back down the hill to disappear until daybreak. The bodies had to be back to the mortuary by daybreak, see, before they were missed by friends and relatives."

"This guy really sounds like a freak."

"Yeah. But I can see how he would get his rocks off playing around with a dead body. It would be kind of a logical extension to his personality, you know? But the

210

others, I couldn't understand how they could enjoy it."

"There were others?"

"Five others. But about halfway through the movie, one of them got murdered."

"No wonder you're still up. Where's this little gem playing?"

"At a little theater in Malibu."

She took a deep swallow of her drink.

"What did you do with the thirty-two, Gloria?"

"Thirty-two? Thirty-two what?"

"Thirty-two caliber pistol. Of the variety used to kill Christopher Ruane."

"I haven't the slightest idea of what you're talking about."

"Let me refresh your memory. You and Christopher Ruane had a little blackmail operation going with the films he had killed your sister and Folsom for, but he started to get shaky and wanted to back out of the deal. He called you late one night and told me he wanted out, and you told him you'd be right over to talk it over. When you got there, you pulled a gun on him and told him he'd better come across with the films. When he didn't, you shot him three times in the chest. Then you ransacked the house looking for them."

"Don't stop now. I've never seen you so amusing."

"You know, my trouble was that I was working backwards. I believed you when you told me your sister had tried to get you interested in the occult when it was actually the other way around. You knew Sascha way before your sister did and the two of you went to work on Sheila's sick attachment to her dead brother to recruit her into Gorman's death-worshipping cult. You knew about the duplicate set of films because your sister told you about them. And as high priestess of the cult, you knew Gorman was

211

sending Ruane to get the films back, so you made a deal with him to kill Folsom and your sister and double-cross Gorman."

"You're missing one vital part, darling. A motive. What motive would I possibly have for all of this?"

"That's another thing that threw me off. I kept working on the angle that Folsom was bumped by somebody he was blackmailing. That tape recording should have tipped me off. There was a cold hatred in it that went way beyond any blackmail motive. What were you going to do—curl up by the fire on cold winter evenings, and listen to your sister die?"

She peered silently into her drink, smiling faintly.

"You're a cool actress, Gloria. But then maybe I was half-blinded by your bed manners. Even that close up I couldn't even see that you were just there to find out if I'd stumbled onto anything. But I don't feel that bad about being taken in. I mean, after all, even your family couldn't read you and they've known you all your life. Your sister couldn't see that you hated her guts with a passion. And your father—that great judge of human nature—couldn't see that you'd love to stick a knife in his back and watch him die. You diluted that ugly hate into a casual indifference and everybody fell for it and it built up and built up until the day you got your chance to let it go.

"There were three things in life your father cared for—money, his good name, and Sheila—and with one sweep of your hand, you took them all away from him. You were going to bleed him white and you were going to make him suffer along the way with the knowledge that his favorite daughter had degenerated into a sleazy tramp. He didn't know that you supervised the degeneration personally and made sure she became everything he despised."

She looked up. Her eyes were empty and black. I had the feeling I was looking all the way to the back of her skull.

"You have ceased to amuse me. Now I would appreciate it if you would put down your drink and rapidly get out of my house before I call the police."

I put the drink down and got up. "Why rush things? They'll probably be calling you soon enough. I dropped a copy of the film off at the Sheriff's Office just about an hour ago. They should be coming around to see you pretty soon. You don't photograph badly at all."

I walked out of the living room and out the front door and down the asphalt driveway to my car. As I turned around, I could see her silhouette against the light of the open door, watching me.

The sky was a dull gray and the first signs of approaching dawn were spreading across the horizon. A couple of birds were chirping somewhere. The air was warming up and it felt like it was going to be a hot summer's day, but that didn't help. Something caught the base of my spine and ran up my back with cold little feet. I shivered as I opened the car door and stepped in.